Passion

Lucas instantly recognized the look in Natalie's eyes because it so perfectly mirrored what he was feeling: hot, blood-boiling passion. She stood there—flushed, furious, provocative—issuing the silent but unmistakable challenge of a woman daring a man to take what she offered.

Lucas had never been one to back down from a challenge. He moved toward her with his gunslinger's walk, slowly, his eyes never leaving hers. He stopped directly in front of her.

Natalie refused to take even one step back. "I told you to leave my house," she said haughtily, then put her hand on the middle of his chest and pushed. "I meant it."

"No, you didn't—" still holding her eyes with his, he took her hand, dragging it slowly down his flat stomach, then lower "—did you?"

He gave her every chance to pull away, but she was utterly still. "No," she agreed softly, "I didn't."

Candace Schuler had fun—and great meals—researching *A Dangerous Game*. She took a course in "How to be a Private Detective," and met several private investigators for lunch. None revealed any details about specific cases, but they provided wonderful ideas for her tenth Temptation novel, *A Dangerous Game*.

Look for Candace's summer 1992 title, *The Mighty Quinn*, in REBELS AND ROGUES, Temptation's celebration of the hero.

Books by Candace Schuler

HARLEQUIN TEMPTATION

Don't miss any of our special offers. Write to us at the following address for information on our newest releases.

Harlequin Reader Service
P.O. Box 1397, Buffalo, NY 14240
Canadian address: P.O. Box 603,
Fort Erie, Ont. L2A 5X3

A Dangerous Game
CANDACE SCHULER

Harlequin Books

TORONTO • NEW YORK • LONDON
AMSTERDAM • PARIS • SYDNEY • HAMBURG
STOCKHOLM • ATHENS • TOKYO • MILAN

To Grace, who worries too much

Published December 1991

ISBN 0-373-25475-X

A DANGEROUS GAME

1

THE AUGUST SKY was a clear, cloudless blue. Lake Minnetonka, lapping gently at the stone breakfront edging the manicured lawn, was smooth and placid, with just enough breeze to send the sailboats and sailboards skimming over its murky green surface. A pair of water bikes, too far away from shore to be heard through the double-paned thermal glass, threw twin rooster-tails of sparkling water into the air.

Standing at the picture window, staring out at the perfect summer afternoon, Natalie Bishop couldn't help but think it was a beautiful day for a gathering of friends and family. She squelched that stray thought immediately, however, feeling guilty for even having let it enter her head; the people in the room behind her weren't gathered to celebrate the beauty of the day, but to mourn the untimely passing of one of their own.

Natalie sighed, reaching up to brush at the thick sheaf of pale blond hair that had fallen over her cheek, and wondered again about what had happened three nights ago, when Rick Peyton met his lonely death.

The facts were simple enough. Sometime between eleven and eleven-thirty on a clear, starlit night, he'd run head-on into an overpass abutment on a long, straight stretch of Highway 494. There had been no other drivers involved and no skid marks to indicate that he had tried to avoid the collision. Because of those simple facts and because, when informed of his death, his widow had made various hysterical comments about her husband's recent "depression" and "all those terrible headaches Ricky's been having lately," the accident was being investigated as a possible suicide by the Minneapolis Police Department.

The autopsy had revealed nothing unusual. There were no drugs in his system except for a large amount of extra-strength aspirin—which seemed to corroborate Sherri Peyton's assertions concerning his headaches—and what amounted to half a pack of Tums still undissolved in his stomach. There'd been barely enough alcohol in his bloodstream to account for the one beer he'd shared with Natalie's brother, Daniel, before leaving work at eight-thirty that evening. Where he'd been between then and the time of his death was still a mystery, but ruling out a drug- or drink-induced accident only strengthened the suspicion of suicide.

And yet . . . Natalie shook her head in silent negation, every instinct she possessed rebelling against believing it. A well-to-do young man in good health with a partnership in an up-and-coming video-game business, married less than a year to a beautiful woman who treated him as if he were a cross between Hugh Hefner and Moses, didn't just up and commit suicide. At least, not in a more perfect world, he didn't.

Not without a reason.

But, then, Natalie thought, still staring out the window, maybe Rick Peyton had had a reason. She hadn't really known him all that well. They hadn't been what anyone could reasonably call friends. He'd just been her younger brother's business partner; a pleasant, if somewhat shallow-seeming young man, with good connections, an expensive education and a nauseatingly perfect little wife.

Not the profile, she reflected again, of someone ripe for suicide—not unless he hadn't been as healthy as he'd seemed, or unless his marriage hadn't been as perfect as it had appeared, or—

"Natalie?" Her brother's voice, pitched low in deference to the occasion, called her from her musings. "Nat, could you come into the den please? Mrs. Peyton—ah, Rick's mother," he added, belatedly remembering there were two Mrs. Peytons present, "would like to speak to you."

Natalie tensed at the summons. Perfect little Sherri Peyton might be the kind of woman every rightthinking feminist would like to stuff into a closet somewhere, but she was essentially harmless. After less than ten minutes in Barbara Peyton's company, however, Natalie had accurately pegged her as the kind of hardas-nails, manipulating man-hater who gave career women everywhere a bad name.

She turned away from the window to answer the summons, nearly running over her older sister, who'd come up behind her. "Oh, Andrea. Sorry," she said. "I didn't mean to step on you." She waved one hand toward the closed door of the den to explain her gracelessness. "Daniel said Mrs. Peyton wants to see me."

"Yes, I heard," Andrea replied in her quiet voice. "I won't keep you. I just wanted to let you know I'm leaving. I have to pick up the kids from the skating rink and then go get the sitter before class." She grimaced. "Her car broke down again."

"I thought you worked nights until September."

"I do. After class."

Natalie peered at her with sisterly concern, noting the fine lines of fatigue around Andrea's eyes. "When do you sleep?"

"Sleep? You mean people still sleep?"

"Andrea . . ."

"I'm only kidding," Andrea said, patting her younger sister's shoulder. "Honest. I get at least, oh, five hours' sleep in every twenty-four."

"Five hours? That isn't nearly enough. You ought—"

"It'll have to be enough for now," Andrea interrupted. "And it won't be for much longer. The kids'll be back in school in a couple of weeks and then I can switch to days."

"While still taking classes at night," Natalie added.

"The sooner I get through these classes, the sooner I can graduate and get my license." Andrea's usually soft expression turned mulish. "And that can't be soon enough for me."

"Yes, but—"

Andrea shook her head impatiently, cutting Natalie off. "I haven't got time to hash this out right now, Nat." She glanced at her watch. "I'm already late."

"You're right. And I'm sorry. You don't need me trying to tell you how to run your life, too." She reached out and hugged her sister lightly. "I didn't mean to nag."

"'S okay," Andrea told her, returning the embrace. She pulled back with a smile. "I know you can't help it."

Natalie watched her sister slip through the few remaining mourners to the front door, silently cursing her sister's ex-husband. After ten years of a marriage in which Andrea had been a dutiful, faithful and loving wife, he'd walked out, leaving her with three children, a house mortgaged to the hilt, an unpaid-for car, no job, and child-support payments that were either late or nonexistent.

Now, three years later, Andrea was just beginning to see a light at the end of the tunnel; and Natalie still envisioned slow torture every time she thought about her ex-brother-in-law.

"Nat?" Daniel prodded. "Mrs. Peyton is waiting."

Natalie sighed and followed her brother into the aggressively masculine little den that had been Rick Peyton's private domain.

Sherri Peyton sat on a tufted leather sofa situated with its back to the curtained glass doors that opened out onto the deck. Her hands were clutched together in her lap, with the mangled hem of a black lace-trimmed hankie peeking out from between her fingers. Her tear-damp face was framed by tendrils of soft reddish hair and the pushed-back net of her widow's veil, making her look, Natalie reflected with an unwelcome spurt of envy, like a dew-kissed rose.

A tall, distinguished man—the lawyer with whom the two Peyton women had been closeted in the den— stood by the desk with his back to the lovely young widow, snapping the locks on an eel-skin briefcase.

The ruthlessly chic, meticulously groomed, expensively preserved elder Mrs. Peyton sat behind what had been her son's desk as if she owned it. Ensconced in his dark green leather chair, she looked more like an annoyed member of upper management than a grieving mother.

"Thank you for your time, Mr. Kemp," Barbara Peyton said to the lawyer. She tapped the papers on the desk in front of her with a bright, brick-red fingernail. "I'll be in touch if there's anything else."

The lawyer nodded and, picking up his briefcase, headed for the door with uncomplimentary haste, angling his body a bit to avoid knocking Natalie over on his way out.

"Come in and close the door, Ms. Bishop," Mrs. Peyton ordered crisply.

Silently doing as she was bidden, Natalie crossed the room to the leather chair in front of the desk. Without giving it any conscious thought, she seated herself near enough to the edge of the chair so her feet would stay on the floor. "What can I do for you, Mrs. Peyton?" she asked, hoping her dislike for the woman wasn't too apparent.

"Sherri tells me you're a private investigator."

"Yes." Natalie crossed her legs, automatically smoothing the skirt of her only dark suit down over her knees. "I am."

Very deliberately, Barbara Peyton let her gaze wander from Natalie's face to her feet and back again, missing no detail of the sleek blond hair, the caramel-colored frames of her stylish glasses that brought out the creaminess of her complexion, the asymmetrically-buttoned forest-green suit, or the impossibly high-heeled pumps on her impossibly small feet. "You won't mind if I say you don't look like a private investigator?" she remarked, raising a skeptical eyebrow.

Natalie shrugged. "Appearances can be deceiving." She knew hers was. Standing a mere five feet, two inches in her bare feet and weighing one hundred and five pounds fully dressed and soaking wet caused a lot of people to underestimate her. But that was their problem, not hers. She'd stopped apologizing for it a long time ago and started using it to her advantage, instead.

"May I ask what kind of experience you have?" Though it was phrased as a polite question, Barbara Peyton's tone made it sound as if she were interviewing Natalie for a job—a very low-paying, menial job.

Natalie opened her mouth, on the verge of answering in a like manner, then decided it wasn't worth the trouble. "I spent almost four years with Shaffer and Associates," she said mildly, naming an agency anyone in the business would recognize as one of the biggest and most prestigious in the Twin Cities. "And I've had my own agency, Strictly Confidential, for the past two and a half years," she added, wondering where the woman was headed. Less than an hour after her son's funeral service hardly seemed the time to be inquiring into someone's business credentials.

"Are you any good?"

Natalie's soft brown eyes narrowed behind the lenses of her oversize glasses. "I'm one of the best," she stated coolly.

"Good." Barbara Peyton acknowledged her show of confidence with a slight, satisfied nod. "Very good," she declared, smiling like a shark about to have lunch. "Because I want you to investigate Lucas."

"Lucas?" Natalie glanced over to where her brother was perched on the arm of the leather sofa next to Sherri. *Lucas who?* her look asked.

Daniel shrugged and spread his hands.

"Lucas Sinclair," Barbara finished. She leaned forward and, resting her elbows on the desk and steepling her hands in front of her, waited until she had everyone's undivided attention. "My other son."

"Your other—" Natalie's eyes widened. "You have another son?"

"From my first marriage."

"I never heard Rick mention a brother." Natalie looked over at Daniel again. "Did you?"

Daniel shook his head.

"He's quite a bit older than Ricky," Barbara told them. "Nearly thirteen years older. I haven't seen him since he left the Marines." Her carefully made-up mouth—the lipstick an exact match for her nails—pursed as if she'd just tasted something particularly nasty. "Apparently, Ricky had. Seen him, that is. Although he never mentioned it to me." She turned a gimlet eye on her daughter-in-law. "Nor did you."

"I only met him once," Sherri offered in a small voice, visibly distressed at the possibility of having angered her formidable mother-in-law.

Daniel reached out and awkwardly patted the widow's shoulder, earning himself a small, grateful smile from Sherri before she explained.

"He was here, in the den, having a drink with Ricky one day when I got back from the grocery store," Sherri said. "Sometime last February, I think. Anyway—" she sniffled and lifted her shoulders in a helpless little shrug "—I fixed them some sandwiches and hot cider and then went back to the kitchen. He left, oh, about a half an hour later, I think. It was starting to snow and he said he wanted to beat the weather. I haven't seen him since then. I just—" she shrugged again "—forgot about him, I guess, and, well . . ." She bit her lip.

"And what?" Barbara demanded.

"And—" Sherri stared down at the hankie she was twisting into knots. "Well . . . Ricky told me not to say anything to, ah . . . anyone."

"Anyone?" Barbara repeated.

"You," Sherri admitted, still staring at her hands. "He said you and Lucas had never gotten along, and knowing he was getting to know his brother would just upset you."

"He was right," Barbara snapped.

Sherri sniffled again, lifting her hankie to her eyes in an obvious effort to block out her mother-in-law's searching gaze.

"I'm not sure I understand what you're after, Mrs. Peyton," Natalie interjected, stepping into the breach to save Sherri from more questioning. "Do you want me to locate your son for you?"

Was it possible, she wondered, that Barbara Peyton wanted to reestablish a relationship with her older son, now that her younger one was lost to her? That she had more maternal feeling than Natalie gave her credit for?

"No, I don't want you to *locate* him," Barbara said, answering Natalie's silent question. "I know where he is." She waved her hand dismissively. "He lives right here in the Twin Cities."

"Well, then," Natalie replied, confused, "if you don't want me to find him, what *do* you want me to do?"

"I want you to investigate him."

"Why?"

"Because he inherited Ricky's share of Galaxies."

"He what?" Natalie and Daniel spoke at once.

Barbara merely lifted one eyebrow, obviously relishing their surprise, then motioned to her daughter-in-law to explain.

Sherri sniffled miserably into her handkerchief before speaking. "Ricky left his shares in Galaxies to Lucas," she said hesitantly, as if she still couldn't quite believe it. "All of them," she added, struggling to control a fresh onslaught of tears. It was a losing battle. "And I hardly even know him!" she wailed, dabbing at her huge cornflower-blue eyes with her mangled hankie.

"And?" Natalie prompted oh-so-gently as Daniel reached over to pat the widow's shoulder again.

"And Sherri's been left destitute!" Barbara announced dramatically.

"Not destitute." Bravely, Sherri pulled herself together to defend her deceased husband. "I have the condo and . . . and the life-insurance money. And my shares of Galaxies—the ones Ricky gave me as a wedding present." She looked at Daniel. "Unless they go to his brother, too, now that Ricky is . . ." She pressed her lips together for a moment to still their trembling.

"Half brother," Barbara reminded them.

"Half brother," Sherri repeated obediently. "Do they?" she asked Daniel.

"No. No, those are yours. I think. That is . . . Rick couldn't have done anything with them without your consent." He looked over at his sister. "Could he?"

Natalie shook her head.

"He couldn't have done anything with them without your consent," Daniel repeated more forcefully. "You didn't give your consent did you? Sign them back or give him power of attorney or something?"

"No."

"Well, then, no matter what he did with the rest of them, those shares are still yours," he declared.

"See?" Sherri said to her mother-in-law. "Ricky didn't leave me destitute."

"As good as. And if the police decide he committed suicide, you won't even have the insurance money," Barbara pointed out with what Natalie thought was unnecessary cruelty. "You'll have to sell this—" she waved a hand, encompassing the entire condo "—just to survive."

Sherri turned the full force of her wide blue eyes on the only man in the room. "Is that true, Danny?" she questioned, reaching out to clutch at his sleeve.

"I, ah...I don't know," Daniel stammered, doing his best to deal with her grief and fear despite his own lingering shock at the suddenness of his partner's death. "Insurance companies usually have some kind of clause about not paying off in cases of, ah—" the word seemed to stick in his throat "—in cases of suicide." He looked at his big sister for help. "Don't they, Nat?"

"Most of the time." Natalie nodded. "But I wouldn't worry about it yet, Sherri," she said gently. "More than likely, it'll turn out to be an accident, pure and simple. They usually are," she added, drawing on her own years of experience as a private investigator, as well as the wisdom gleaned from her father's sixteen years with the Minneapolis police force. The simplest scenario usually turned out to be the right one. She hoped it was true in this case.

"Do you think so?" Sherri was still looking to Daniel for confirmation. "Do you *really* think so?"

Daniel did his best to look authoritative. "If Nat says that's the way it is, then that's probably the way it is," he said, patting the hand that still clutched his sleeve.

"And in the meantime, a total stranger is in control of what should rightfully be Sherri's future," Barbara burst out angrily.

"Certainly not a total stranger," Natalie countered. "He *is* your son."

"Whom I haven't seen in over ten years," Barbara snapped. "I had no idea Ricky had seen him, either—"

she sniffed disdainfully "—let alone borrowed money from him."

"Why would Ricky borrow money from his brother?" Natalie demanded.

"*Half* brother," Barbara again corrected. "As to why he borrowed money from Lucas, I'm sure I don't know."

"The lawyer said he borrowed money from his br— half brother—" Sherri caught herself with a quick glance at Barbara "—to finance some sort of expansion at Galaxies. The lawyer said Ricky used his shares for, ah—" her lovely forehead puckered "—collateral, I think he said."

"Expansion?" Natalie asked, looking at her brother.

"Rick had been talking about doing more advertising. He said we were at the point where we needed to do some really eye-catching stuff if we wanted to grow beyond a Mom-and-Pop kind of operation. You know—big, splashy ads in the most popular video magazines, a booth at some of the trade shows, things like that. I guess he'd decided to go ahead with it," Daniel told them, without much certainty. The business end of Galaxies was strictly up to Rick; Daniel's expertise was in developing the video games Galaxies sold.

"Well, if he needed money, he could have borrowed it from me," Barbara huffed. "Why didn't he come to me?"

"I don't know," Sherri said.

But Natalie had a very good idea what his reason might have been. Taking money from his mother would have meant dancing at the end of her string; and Rick Peyton had apparently been smarter than that.

"So," Natalie interjected, drawing everyone's attention back to the original question under discussion, "you want me to investigate your son," she said to Barbara Peyton. "And then—" she spread her hands "—what exactly?"

"I want you to *get* something on him," Barbara declared fiercely. "Something so that I—" her glance shifted over to her daughter-in-law "—we," she corrected smoothly, smiling at Sherri "—so that *we* can force him to sign those shares back over to Sherri, where they rightfully belong."

And where you can control them, Natalie added silently.

"It shouldn't be too difficult," Barbara went on. "Lucas was an incorrigible child and he only got worse as he got older. He was always in trouble for one thing or another. Cutting school, shoplifting, getting caught in the back seat of a car with some trashy girl—that sort of thing." She paused, picking at a nonexistent piece of thread on the front of her black designer suit jacket as if to underscore the fact that her son's behavioral problems were of no more concern than the inconvenience they'd put her to. "He even stole a car once. We—Ricky's father and I—were ready to put him in juvenile hall over that one, but he saved us the trouble by running away."

Coldhearted bitch, Natalie thought, feeling all her sympathy going out to the unknown Lucas. No one, no matter how "incorrigible," deserved a woman like

Barbara Peyton for a mother. Natalie allowed none of her feelings to show however, as she returned the older woman's cool gaze.

"I doubt the threat of having a few juvenile offences exposed would make anyone amenable to—" Natalie hesitated and then decided to call a spade a spade "—blackmail," she pronounced silkily, wondering if Barbara Peyton would deny that that was exactly what she had in mind.

She didn't. "People don't change," she argued. "Lucas was a no-good hell-raiser and a womanizer when he was seventeen and I have no doubt he still is. Surely, if you look hard enough, Ms. Bishop, you'll find something even Lucas would be ashamed to have the whole world know about him."

2

ON THE DECK, just outside the half-open sliding-glass doors, Lucas Sinclair stood listening to his mother denigrate him, totally amazed that her words could still, after all this time, wound him. Not so deeply as they had when he was seventeen, of course. Nor as they had when, at age twenty-six, he'd come home from the Marines with a new wife and a new life and the mistaken belief that his mother—then a widow with another teenage son to raise—would be as eager to make amends and start over as he. No, nothing could hurt him that deeply again, and yet . . .

Deliberately Lucas uncurled his fingers, telling himself that his reaction to her words was only the very natural reaction of anyone hearing himself being called "no good" and then being set up for exactly what the little sexpot blonde had called it.

Blackmail.

He could feel the hot, hurting emotion boiling up, just the way it had when he was seventeen years old and enraged by yet another example of his mother's total lack of maternal regard for him.

But he knew how to control that feeling now, how to direct it. How to tamp it down and channel it into a more useful outlet than an emotional explosion—*that* would have been the reaction of the boy who'd run away to join the Marines. He took a deep, calming breath, then another and another, until the emotion that had almost swamped him was well below the surface. Then, curving his lips into a small, deliberate smile, Lucas pushed aside the curtain and stepped quietly into the room.

He was immensely gratified—in a perverse sort of way, he supposed—to see his mother's startled reaction. It was her first sight of him in over ten years. Her eyes widened; her mouth fell open; the blood drained from her face. He waited, still as a stalking cat, until the other occupants of the room turned to see what had caused Barbara Peyton to turn ghost-white beneath her expertly applied makeup.

The sexy little blonde was first, her head turning so quickly that her hair swung against her cheek. His brother's boy-genius business partner was next, his wide forehead screwed up in a puzzled frown as he swiveled around to see what the blonde was looking at. And then, finally, Rick's lovely, fragile widow, her big blue eyes damp with suppressed tears, turned her head to look up at him.

Lucas glanced briefly at them all before nodding curtly to the woman sitting white-faced and stock-still behind the desk where he'd last seen his half brother. "Hello, Mother," he said, his smile cooling a shade when she flinched.

Another fifteen seconds of strained silence passed in slow motion as everyone waited to see what would happen next.

Well, the heartless old witch is at last half right Natalie thought as she stared at the silent intruder in their midst. *Her son is definitely a hell-raiser.*

Thanks in part to her father, who'd been a hell-raiser himself in his day, and to the men she met in the course of her work, she knew the type all too well. Lucas Sinclair had all the earmarks of an aggressively macho male.

Oh, he's a hell-raiser, all right.

His dark brown hair was cut just a bit too short to be fashionable, hinting at a Marine past that wasn't as far behind him as the years would lead one to believe. His nose had a crook in it, the kind that suggested it had been broken—more than once, probably; and then not seen to as soon as it should have been. His startlingly-pale green eyes held a cynical seen-it-all gleam. His smile was cool and sardonic, involving nothing more than the curve of his lips. But it was the way he stood that really revealed his hell-raising tendencies. He had a gunslinger's stance—relaxed, easy and go-to-hell arrogant on the surface; tense, wary and ready for anything underneath.

Definitely a hell-raiser, Natalie reflected again, and then wondered if Barbara had been right about her son's womanizing, as well; it was a very real possibility. Lucas Sinclair's angular, lived-in face, his heavy boxer's shoulders and mess-with-me-if-you-dare body language would be infinitely more interesting than glossy good looks to any number of women. Herself included, Natalie acknowledged privately, silently bemoaning her unfortunate—albeit well-hidden—weakness for macho, steely-eyed, Clint Eastwood types, despite the trouble they caused the female half of the population.

Daniel, meanwhile, was shifting his puzzled gaze back and forth between Natalie and Rick Peyton's half brother. He was clearly wondering about the man, but just as clearly, he was waiting for his sister's reaction before making any judgments of his own.

Sherri Peyton just sat there on the sofa, round-eyed with shock, and stared at the man she'd seen only once before in her life. The man who, now—if the lawyer and her mother-in-law were to be believed—held her future in his hands.

Finally, Barbara Peyton broke the tense, expectant stillness. Very deliberately, she leaned back in her chair. "What are you doing here?" she demanded of her son, sounding very much as if she thought he'd come to steal the silver.

Lucas's cool smile didn't waver. "Basically the same thing you are, I imagine," he replied. "Paying my respects to Rick's widow."

"Come to claim the spoils, is more like it," his mother retorted.

Lucas inclined his head. "As I said. Basically the same thing you are." Then, pointedly ignoring her look of outrage, he reached over the back of the leather sofa and touched Sherri's shoulder.

She jumped as if she'd been scalded.

"I'm sorry." His voice held a surprising gentleness. "Terribly sorry for your loss."

Sherri's lips trembled pathetically.

"I was only just getting to know Rick myself," Lucas continued, hoping she wasn't going to break down in hysterical tears, and yet, approving of her lack of control over her emotions. It was so typically feminine, and there were far too few truly feminine women left in the modern world. "What little I knew of him, though, I liked," he said. It wasn't precisely true. There were certain aspects of Rick's personality he hadn't liked at all, but that wasn't important right now. Offering a few words of comfort to Rick's grieving widow was. "I want you to know you won't have to sell anything to—" he gave a quick, sardonic glance at his mother "—survive," he assured her. "No matter what happens."

"Thank you." Sherri dabbed at her eyes and smiled tremulously through her tears, immediately comforted by the promise implicit in his words.

"Does that mean you're signing those shares back over to her?" Barbara asked.

"No, Mother. It doesn't." His tone was a startling contrast to the gentle one he'd used with Sherri. "Rick left his shares to me for a reason." *So you wouldn't get your greedy hands on them, no doubt.* "I intend to find out what that reason was before I do anything at all."

He came around the sofa as he spoke and held his hand out to Daniel. "Lucas Sinclair," he said, as if everyone in the room weren't already well aware of who he was. "It looks like we're going to be partners. For a while, at least."

"Yes, it does." Daniel stood, glancing at Natalie before reaching out to shake the offered hand. "Pleased to meet you," he responded as good manners won out over caution.

"I only wish it could have been under different circumstances," Lucas remarked, not missing the uneasy look the younger man had given his . . . what? Girlfriend? Wife? He turned to where the blonde still sat, her gaze boldly assessing him from behind the oversize lenses of her glasses. "And you are?" he asked bluntly, immediately classifying her as another one of those pushy, aggressive "modern" women, just like his ex-wife—and his mother.

She stood and offered her hand in a no-nonsense, businesslike fashion, confirming his assessment of her. "Natalie Bishop," she answered crisply, quite used to dealing with men on an equal basis, even if the man in question wasn't. "Daniel's sister," she added, just so there would be no confusion, then felt like kicking herself for giving in to the impulse. She didn't care if he knew whether she was married or not!

So, she's his sister, Lucas thought, trying to deny the spurt of satisfaction the knowledge gave him. He took her hand in as brisk and businesslike a manner as she offered it, looking down—way down—at her as he did so.

Her gaze was sharp and direct as she looked back at him, full of hard questions and blatant speculation. Her grip was as firm as any young man's. But her sleek blond head barely came to the top of his shoulder, despite the lethal height of her heels. Her eyes, behind the lenses of the fashionable glasses and the facade of cool speculation, were as big and soft and brown as a cocker spaniel's. Her hand, for all its firmness, was appealingly small and soft in his. And, on top of everything else, she was wearing perfume. Something feminine and floral with undertones of sexy Oriental spice, deliberately designed to hit a man where he lived.

Oh, this is just great! Lucas thought sourly, feeling himself drawn to her against his will. Why in *hell* did she have to be exactly like the type of woman he was most physically attracted to? It was damn unfair. *Damn* unfair! Modern career women should look like career women, not like his fantasy of the perfect bedmate!

Natalie glanced down at their hands, intending, by her pointed expression, to let him know he'd been holding hers too long. Instead, she found herself staring.

He had a tattoo on the back of his hand. The sleek head of a cobra, deadly and beautiful, snaked out from beneath the cuff of his crisp white shirt, its forked tongue extended as if testing to see whether it was safe to emerge.

Another souvenir of his hell-raising Marine past, she surmised, as a shiver of something deliciously thrilling slid down her spine and lodged itself in the most feminine recesses of her body. *Oh, no!* she thought in the next instant, trying to deny she'd felt anything at all.

It was no use. Despite her oft-expressed and truly felt admiration for the gentleness and sensitivity of the "new age" male, she'd always had an unhealthy appreciation for a man with a hint—all right, more than a hint!—of danger about him. Alarmed, she pulled her hand out of his with a sharp tug.

"How did you know about the shares?" she asked briskly in an effort to negate and erase her embarrassing reaction.

"The what?" he murmured, wondering what kind of trouble she was going to cause him. He didn't doubt for a minute that she would; women like her *always* caused trouble, especially for men like him. It often seemed to him that they went out of their way to cause trouble.

"The shares." Natalie felt tiny and defenseless and deliciously, helplessly female as he continued to stand there, towering over her, staring down at her with an intent, angry light in his pale green eyes. Resolutely she pushed her feelings away and stiffened her spine against their return. "We just learned about the way Rick left the shares a little while ago," she continued more forcefully. "So how did you know that you and Daniel are partners?"

"Obviously he was eavesdropping," Barbara said nastily, flinging out a hand toward the glass doors.

"Partly," Lucas acknowledged, managing, at last, to turn away from Natalie and face his mother. Sexy little Natalie Bishop wasn't his type, he told himself sternly, no matter what she looked like, and that was that! "I also had a message on my answering machine from a Mr. Kemp," he continued, "suggesting that since I was the principal heir, I might like to be present at the reading of my brother's will." He paused. "It was the first I'd heard about his death."

Daniel whistled softly. "Hell of a way to find out," he muttered.

Natalie agreed. It was an appalling way to find out about the death of a brother, even a half brother you were just getting to know, or even— Her mind skittered to an abrupt stop and began backtracking.

Had Lucas Sinclair really "only just been getting to know" his younger half-brother? After all, there weren't many people who'd lend money to someone they barely knew, even if the borrower was a relative. She smiled grimly. *Especially* if the borrower was a relative. It was a sure-fire road to disaster, her father always said. A man as worldly-wise and cynical as Lucas Sinclair appeared to be would know that. Unless . . .

She glanced at him as he stood—cool, controlled and as dangerous as a live specimen of the cobra coiled around his wrist—trading icy stares with his mother.

Unless he expected to get something out of it, Natalie finished her thought. Something besides the interest on a loan of— How much money were they talking about here, anyway? Hundreds? Thousands? Hundreds of thousands? It had to be a considerable amount, she realized with a start, to warrant putting an entire partnership up as collateral. But how much could a few advertisements in a computer hackers' magazine cost? Surely not—

"I'll just bet!" Barbara burst out suddenly, bringing an abrupt end to Natalie's frantic musings, and to the staring contest between herself and Lucas. "I'll just bet it's the first you've heard about all this." She came to her feet and leaned across the desk, planting her hands flat on its shiny surface as she confronted her son. "I think you planned it," she accused.

Daniel gasped softly.

Natalie stiffened, shocked to her bones at the implication in Barbara Peyton's words.

"Planned it?" Sherri echoed naively from her seat on the sofa. "Planned what?"

Lucas refined the question. "Yes, M—" He broke off, unable to bring himself to call her Mother just then, not even with the sardonic edge he usually gave the word. "Yes," he prodded, his voice low and menacing, "tell us what it is you think I planned?"

"I think my meaning is quite clear."

"Humor me," he challenged. His soft, too-smooth voice raised the hairs on the back of Natalie's neck and caused Barbara to retreat from her aggressive stance over the desk. "Spell it out so there's no mistake."

Barbara took a step backward, suddenly at a loss for words.

Lucas took a corresponding step forward. "Well?" he demanded. "We're waiting."

"All right." Barbara lifted her head defiantly, throwing caution to the winds. "All right, then, I will! It's no secret that Ricky died under—" she took a shaky breath "—under suspicious circumstances, and—"

"Suspicious?" Sherri interrupted. "There was nothing sus—"

Daniel put a hand on her shoulder to keep her still.

"Under suspicious circumstances," Barbara repeated, ignoring her daughter-in-law's outburst and the hard, implacable expression on her son's face. "There were no skid marks. No drugs or alcohol in his bloodstream. Nothing at all to indicate that what happened was just an accident."

"Then what was it?" Lucas demanded.

"The police think it was suicide."

"No," Sherri countered. "No, it was an accident."

"Hush," Daniel said, and squeezed her shoulder.

"But—"

"Hush," he repeated.

"What do you think it was?" Lucas asked his mother. The low-voiced question vibrated as dangerously as unsheathed steel. His pale green eyes glittered. His body was as still as a cobra waiting to strike.

Like a gunslinger in a saloon, Natalie thought, *squaring off across a poker table with the player who'd called him a cheat.* She had to still an impulse to dive for cover.

"What do you think it was?" Lucas asked again when Barbara didn't answer.

Murder? Natalie wondered. *Would she come right out and say she thought it was murder?*

It was pure nonsense, of course. Pure, unadulterated, spiteful nonsense. And yet... Natalie couldn't quite silence the voice of experience reminding her that greed was a powerful motive for a lot of things—fratricide most definitely included. And the plain, unassailable fact was, Lucas Sinclair had gained a great deal by his brother's death.

But murder? Natalie asked herself again, strangely unwilling to consider it in connection with Lucas Sinclair, no matter how dangerous he appeared at the moment.

"Suicide," Barbara stated finally. "I think it was suicide."

Natalie let out a breath she hadn't known she'd been holding.

"But I think you had a hand in it," Barbara added, erasing the mitigating effect of her last statement. "I think that, somehow, some way, you drove him to it."

Lucas's broad shoulders twitched as if he'd just taken a blow. "Drove him to it!" He slammed his hands flat on the smooth surface of the desk, looming over it as if he might, at any minute, leap over it. "Drove him to it!" he repeated, the growl in his voice sounding like thunder on the horizon. "Just what in hell do you mean by that?"

Barbara shrank under the fierceness of his expression, sitting down abruptly in the leather chair behind her. She curled her fingers around the arms of the chair and her knuckles turned white. "Just exactly what I said," she insisted stubbornly, displaying what Natalie considered to be foolhardy courage in the face of her son's steely-eyed rage. "I think you loaned him the money, knowing full well he'd never be able to pay it back. Knowing that sooner or later, he'd have to default. And, then, when he did, I think you hounded him and badgered him until he couldn't think straight—until he didn't know where to turn or what to do. Sherri said he'd been distracted and depressed lately, and I think—"

"You think!" Lucas mimicked her. "And do you know why you think that way... *Mother*" The word was infused with a lifetime of pain and anger. "I'll tell you why! Because that's exactly what *you* would have done!"

Barbara surged to her feet, pushing the chair away with the backs of her legs to give herself room. "But *I* didn't," she accused. "You did. *You* drove him to suicide!"

"No!" Sherri shook off Daniel's restraining hand and lunged to her feet. "No, Ricky didn't kill himself!"

Lucas moved before anyone could react. Whirling around, he caught Sherri before she'd taken two steps. She struggled against him for a moment, causing her little veiled hat to tumble off, and then collapsed in a teary heap against his chest.

"Ricky *didn't* kill himself," she repeated, sobbing. "It was an accident...an accident." Still clenching the tear-damp hankie, she pounded her small fist against his broad chest. "An accident."

"Yes." He held her gently, his big hand with its cobra tattoo tenderly cupping the back of her head, his other arm around her shoulders, cradling her as tenderly as if she were a child. "It was an accident," he crooned, hoping he was right, and vowing that he'd find out exactly what was behind his brother's death if there was more to it than simple, unforgiving chance. "It was just an accident."

The phone rang then—a shrill sound that overrode Lucas's surprisingly soothing voice. His mother reached for it automatically. "Barbara Peyton here," she answered, then said, "It's for you." She held the receiver out to Natalie.

Gingerly, her gaze still fixed on Lucas and Sherri, Natalie took the phone from her. "Hello? Dad? What are you doing calling— Are you sure? No." She shook her head. "No, I'm sorry, Dad. Of course, you're sure. You wouldn't have called if you weren't. Yes, I'll tell them." She leaned over and, very gently, put the receiver into its cradle. "That was my father," she announced, staring down at her hand on the phone. "He was calling from the station. They've finished going over the car."

"And?" Lucas prompted, his voice—his whole body—tense.

"It wasn't suicide."

"Thank God!"

"Rick's car had been tampered with." She looked up, directly into Lucas Sinclair's pale green eyes. "The police think he was murdered."

3

"COME ON, DAD, cut me some slack." Natalie sat perched on her father's desk, hands braced on either side of her hips, legs crossed at the ankles. "It isn't going to go any farther than right here."

"And what about Barbara Peyton? I heard she hired you to investigate her son." He gave his daughter a sharp look. "Blackmail was what I heard."

Natalie's look was equally sharp. "You know better than that, Dad."

"Yeah," he admitted. "I guess I do." He dropped his gaze back to the folder on the desk in front of him.

"Then you'll help me get the information?" She leaned in, prepared to do some serious wheedling if necessary. "You know I wouldn't ask if it wasn't important."

"And you know you shouldn't be asking me at all," her father replied gruffly, continuing to read from the open folder. "No matter what the reason."

She leaned in closer. "But this is a really *good* reason, Dad," she continued sweetly, keeping her voice low in deference to the other police officers, station workers, and assorted complainants, miscreants and felons who inhabited her father's workplace. "You know it is."

Nathan Bishop looked up from under bushy gray eyebrows without lifting his head. "No matter what the reason," he repeated.

Natalie straightened. "But—"

"No buts, little girl." He sighed heavily to show his daughter just how much she was annoying him and how forbearing he was being about it, then closed the folder, setting it aside to deal with her in a more direct fashion. "You know as well as I do that juvenile records can't be opened without a judge's order. Which I know you don't have—"

"Yet."

"—because you would have flashed it, first thing, instead of trying to sweet-talk your way around your old man," he said, letting her know he'd seen through her act.

Natalie didn't even have the grace to look guilty at being caught using her feminine wiles; she firmly believed that one should use what one had, even on one's father. "I can get one if I have to," she insisted stubbornly.

Her father shook his graying head. "Not likely. And you know it. No judge worth his salt is going to let you open sealed records just to satisfy your curiosity about some guy you think *might* have had something to do with his brother's murder. And if I ever hear about one doing it—" his eyes held a glitter of warning; there was nothing that riled Lieutenant Nathan Bishop more than people who betrayed positions of public trust "—I'll do my damnedest to nail his butt to the wall. And yours, too."

"It isn't just curiosity," Natalie defended herself, wisely focusing on the lesser of the sins of which she'd just been accused. "And I didn't say he had anything to do with his brother's murder," she argued, because she hadn't. And wouldn't. Merely thinking of Lucas Sinclair and murder together in the same sentence was disturbing enough; she would never actually say it out loud. "I just wanted to do a background check on him, is all," she said, smoothing a hand over the skirt of her bright teal-blue suit. "A perfectly legal background check. He *is* going to be Daniel's business partner. For a while, anyway." She gave her father an accusing, narrow-eyed stare from behind her glasses. "I'd think you'd want to check up on him yourself. You know how Daniel is."

"Yes, I know how Daniel is," Nathan agreed.

Father and daughter smiled at each other. Head-in-the-ozone Daniel, with his genius for all things electronic, his fascination with "sword and sorcery," and his complete lack of practicality regarding everything else, was a bit of a puzzle to the more pragmatic members of his family. That being the case, they felt it was up to them to protect him—from himself, if necessary.

"Which is why I've already done a little checking on this Lucas fella of yours."

"He isn't *my* Lucas fella," Natalie corrected quickly. Too quickly. "Now, don't go looking at me like that, Dad," she warned sternly. "I was just stating a simple fact. Lucas Sinclair isn't of any interest to me beyond his involvement in this case," she lied. "So just cut it out."

"What?" her father asked innocently. "What did I do?"

Natalie gave him a look that said he knew exactly what he'd done.

"Well, you can't blame your old father for hoping, can you?" he grumbled. "Daughter nearly gone on twenty-six and no one to take care of her yet."

"You mean the way Kevin took care of Andrea?" she said sweetly, referring to her sister's ex-husband.

Nathan Bishop gave his daughter a pained look. "Don't you worry about Andrea. She'll find someone better than that low-life snake to take care of her before you will."

"I don't need anyone to take care of me," she replied, wondering why she bothered; it was an old argument and neither of them was likely to have a change of opinion. "And neither does Andrea."

"All women need someone to take care of them. It's the natural order of things."

Natalie put her hands over her ears. "I'm not listening to this."

Her father opened his mouth as if to say more, then shut it again and reached out, instead, pushing the file he'd been reading across the scarred surface of the desk with the tip of his index finger. "Might as well take a look," he invited, nudging it against his daughter's hip.

Natalie lowered her hands. "You mean it's his?"

Her father nodded.

"Why, you old fox, you," she said, instantly forgiving. She snatched up the file, flipping it open with a flick of her wrist. "There isn't much here."

"There's enough."

"Humph." Natalie settled herself more comfortably on the edge of the desk, recrossing her nylon-clad legs at the knee, and began to read. "A couple of parking tickets," she observed, as she skimmed the top sheet. "Plus a couple of appearances in court for..." She read silently for a minute or two. "For the D.A. as a computer expert!" She rolled her eyes at that piece of information. "He and Daniel ought to get along just peachy keen," she commented. "But—" she breathed a small, grateful sigh "—it's not much of a record."

"Keep reading," her father advised. "It's actually a hell of a record."

She gave him a long, searching look over the rims of her glasses and then flipped to the next page. "'Nine years in the Marines,'" she read aloud. "'Division boxing champion. Volunteered for two tours in Nam. Field promotion to captain. Three Purple Hearts. A Silver Star.' With clusters, no less. 'Distinguished Service Medal.' Impressive," she remarked, trying not to be too impressed and failing miserably. Bona fide heroes always impressed her; she'd gotten all her values from a man who'd spent his life serving his country, both in and out of the Marines.

"He was in the thick of it when Saigon fell," her father said. "Got shot up pretty bad loading some refugees onto a helicopter, but managed to get them all safely away, anyhow."

Natalie looked up over the edge of the folder at her father. "It doesn't say that here."

"I called an old buddy in D.C."

"Oh, I see. It's okay for you to use contacts and pull strings to get a file, but not for me, huh?"

"A man's military records aren't sealed."

"They aren't exactly a matter of public record, either."

Her father shrugged.

Natalie went back to reading Lucas Michael Sinclair's military file. As her father had said, it was a hell of a record, if not exactly what she'd been expecting. "Got his degree in computer technology after Vietnam, then went back on active duty in the intelligence division doing . . ." She looked up over the edge of the folder again. "There's a whole paragraph here that's been completely blacked out."

"There are some strings even your old man can't pull."

"Top-secret spy stuff?"

"Maybe."

"Secret messages and meetings at midnight?" she suggested, intrigued in spite of herself. "Opposite numbers in the KGB? That kind of spy stuff?"

Nathan shook his head. "You're more like your brother than I thought," he commented, amused.

"Double-oh-seven and a license to—" The teasing note faded from her voice as she realized what she was about to say. "—kill?"

"Try decoding computer cryptographics in some dingy, windowless office," said a voice next to her ear, "and you'd be closer to the mark."

Natalie whirled around so fast she nearly fell off the desk. Lucas reached out, casually placing a hand under her elbow to steady her.

"What are you doing here?" she demanded, jerking her arm out of his hand. The file went flying, landing on the floor by her father's chair.

"I was invited," Lucas said mildly, trying not to stare too hard at her legs. They were awfully long for such a little bit of a thing, and her position on the desk—not to mention the high-heeled, ankle-strap hooker shoes she had on—showcased them to spectacular, mouth-watering advantage.

"Invited by whom?" Natalie asked suspiciously, resisting the urge to tug her skirt down over her knees.

"By me, little girl," Nathan answered as he leaned over to retrieve the file.

Natalie frowned at the top of her father's head; it was bad enough that he called her "little girl" at all, but doing it in front of Lucas Sinclair was outside of enough. It made her feel...little and feminine and as delicate as one of the porcelain figurines Andrea used to collect. It also made her mad.

Not that either of the two men noticed her miffed expression. Or would have been bothered by it if they had.

They were two of a kind, she realized, looking back and forth between them: overly macho males who firmly believed a woman's place was in the home and under a masculine thumb. An indulgent, benevolent thumb, to be sure, but a thumb nonetheless.

"I got your message on my machine, sir," Lucas said as the older man straightened with the folder in his hand.

Natalie watched him slide up another notch or two in her father's estimation with the word *sir*. She wondered if that's why he'd used it. Ten years, after all, was a long time to retain a habit of address, and if there was one way to impress an ex-Marine, it was to remind him that you were one, too.

"You said you wanted to talk to me at my earliest convenience," Lucas continued. "So, here I am."

"You didn't have to come all the way downtown, Captain Sinclair." Nathan leaned back in his chair and tossed the folder onto his desk. "I think we could have handled the whole thing over the phone."

"Probably," Lucas agreed. "But I have a few questions of my own that need answering. And it's just plain Lucas Sinclair, sir," he added, extending his hand. The cobra slithered into plain sight. "I haven't been called Captain for more than ten years."

"Lucas." Nathan nodded, standing to shake the offered hand. "And it's Nate to an ex-marine." Their hands fell apart. "Well, sit down. Sit down." He looked at his daughter as if he'd just realized she was still perched on the edge of his desk. "Get down from there, Natalie," he told her with good-natured annoyance, "and go away. Lucas and I have police business to discuss."

"Go right ahead." Natalie smiled with saccharine sweetness, tearing her gaze from the fascinating tattoo on the back of Lucas's hand to glare at her father. "Don't mind me."

"*Official* police business," Nathan insisted. "As in, none of your business."

"It's just as much my business as it is—" she began indignantly, only to break off as she felt Lucas's hands around her waist.

"Allow me," he said, lifting her off the desk as if she weighed no more than a child.

For just the briefest second, their bodies touched. It was a fleeting brush of cloth against cloth, a mere hint of hard against soft, a tantalizing suggestion of man against woman—the faintest whisper of elemental heat. They both felt it to their toes.

And they both would have denied it to their last breath.

"Well," Natalie stated huffily, hiding her confusion—and her adroit appropriation of Lucas's file—by making a show of hurrying. "I guess I'll be going, then." She gave her father a level look. "I can find out what I want to know somewhere else." It was a subtle threat, a reminder that the woman he indulgently dismissed as a "little girl" wasn't without resources of her own.

"It might not be as easy as you think," her father pointed out. "Jeffries isn't in Records anymore."

Natalie raised a delicate eyebrow. "Meaning?"

"The last time you batted your eyelashes at him, he let you make copies of files you had no business even looking at. I thought it was in his best interests to be transferred to an environment with less temptation."

Natalie drew herself up to her full height. "I do *not* bat my eyelashes!" she retorted furiously. Turning on a teal-blue heel, she stalked out of the squad room with as much dignity as a woman could muster in three-inch spikes.

There was a moment of appreciative silence as both men watched her slam through the swing doors.

"She does, though," Nathan said, with that half-amused, half-admiring air common to men who have angered their womenfolk just to watch the fireworks and then gotten a bit more than they bargained for. "Thing is, she doesn't even know she does it."

"Sir?" Lucas questioned absently, his eyes straining for a last glimpse of Natalie's furiously twitching hips.

"Bat her eyelashes."

"Oh, Lord, yes." Lucas laughed. "Don't they all."

NATALIE FUMED all the way to Records where indeed, Jeffries no longer worked. The officer behind the desk was a veteran, unimpressed by the various stratagems employed to wheedle information out of public officials. Wisely, Natalie didn't even try to talk the woman into releasing the forbidden files. She headed over to where the county records were housed instead—since she had to go over there on another case, anyway—intent on digging up any documents on Lucas Michael Sinclair that were a simple matter of public record. She was determined to find, as his mother had said, *something* with which to make him squirm.

Three hours of digging through files and staring at microfiche didn't give her much to work with.

There was the usual, easily obtainable information on his early years. Born on a winter's day at Methodist Hospital, Lucas Sinclair had been a big baby, weighing in at healthy nine pounds four ounces. His mother had been a secretary at Peyton Office Supply; his father an unemployed construction worker. Judging from the divorce decree, dated when Lucas would have been barely eight months old, and the subsequent legal notices suing for payment of child support and alimony, it looked as if Barbara Sinclair—eventually-to-be Peyton—may have had some legitimate reasons for her bitterness toward men.

Records on Lucas past the sixth grade were nonexistent, and those available after his teen years weren't particularly enlightening. Doggedly, Natalie made notes on what there was.

He was a registered Republican.

He purchased a yearly fishing license.

He owned a boat trailer, a modest-size powerboat, a snowmobile and a 1988 Jeep Cherokee wagon, which she already knew about, having seen him drive it away from Sherri Peyton's lakeside condo.

He paid all his county licenses, registration fees and taxes promptly and in full.

He was the sole owner and stockholder of a company called Sinclair Security, Inc. Its main business, spelled out in some detail in its state charter, had to do with highly sophisticated computer systems that guarded other computer systems against being broken into by casual hackers and/or deliberate felons. He apparently also designed and installed the more usual types of security systems for homes and businesses.

It looked as if he'd found a profitable use for the cryptographic skills he'd picked up working for military intelligence, she thought as she jotted down the pertinent facts in her own unique brand of shorthand. Not that she believed computer skills were all he'd learned. Not by a long shot. A man's military records weren't classified because he'd done a little simple code-cracking for Uncle Sam. There had to be some really *interesting* information buried in that blacked-out paragraph—information she'd give her favorite pair of shoes to obtain.

She was still speculating on what it could be as she systematically exchanged one strip of microfiche for another, even though she really didn't expect to find anything of interest here.

But she did.

Married, she observed with something very like dismay as she automatically jotted down the information.

He and a woman named Madeline Stratton had purchased a marriage license in 1981.

The newlyweds had purchased a modest house in a high-rent suburb of Minneapolis in 1982.

And— *Ah, this is more like it!*—she filed for divorce in 1984. Citing "irreconcilable differences," she'd asked for, and gotten, the house, one of the two cars registered to Mr. and Ms. Stratton-Sinclair, but no alimony or child support.

The last bit of information she dug up was a deed. Lucas Sinclair owned a house out on one of the westernmost shorelines of Lake Minnetonka—the very same lake on which his brother also owned a home. It was a small house, according to the deed, but he'd added on to it—quite a lot, judging by the number of building permits he'd obtained over the years—and twelve acres of prime lakefront property went with it. Natalie filed that tidbit away with the rest of the information she gleaned and then, confident she'd ferreted out every bit of information available on Lucas Sinclair, turned her attention to the two other cases she was currently working on.

Both of them—a suspected arson and a suspiciously large property loss on an insurance claim—were routine but time-consuming. It was late when she left the building and she was hungry. She decided to go to the nearest fast-food restaurant for a bite to eat before heading over to Galaxies.

It was probably a long shot, but maybe she would find something in Rick Peyton's files and records that would indicate more clearly just exactly what part his half brother had really played in his life.

LUCAS LEFT the Minneapolis Police Department feeling both better and worse then he had before the meeting with Natalie Bishop's father. Better, because he'd managed to convince Nate Bishop—not that it had taken much convincing—that he'd had nothing to do with his half brother's death. Worse, because he now knew just as much as the Minneapolis police did about how Rick had died, and it most definitely hadn't been by accident.

What the police department still didn't know was who had tampered with Rick's car, and why.

The questions ate at Lucas like a cancer. Could it possibly have had something to do with the twenty thousand dollars he'd loaned his young brother last February?

To say he'd been surprised when Rick called him out of the blue, asking if they could meet, would be to understate the case by a significant degree. They hadn't seen each other in almost twenty years. He'd been seventeen, which would have made Rick all of four years old at the time. *Hell*, Lucas thought, yanking at the knot in his tie as he made his way through the parking lot to his black Cherokee, he'd almost forgotten he had a brother. He'd have given odds that, young as he'd been, Rick wouldn't have remembered him at all.

That being the case, Lucas had been both leery and intrigued on that December afternoon when he picked up the phone to hear a voice claiming to be from his past. Rick had been diffident but warm, apologizing for calling but making it clear he felt it was time—and past time—that the two brothers met again.

"I got married last summer," he'd explained, "and we've been talking about starting a family. It got me to thinking how, well . . . I ought to get to know the family I have first."

They'd met a couple of times at bars and restaurants and, finally, at Rick's home. Both of them tacitly acknowledged the wisdom of keeping their budding relationship from their mother, at least until they'd decided just exactly how much of a relationship it was going to be.

They'd known each other less than three months before Rick brought up the matter of a loan.

Lucas had realized immediately that he'd been manipulated. But he went along with it. Partly because he had the money—the security business paid extremely well. Partly out of a nagging sense of unresolved guilt for having resented the much younger brother who'd gotten all the maternal devotion he hadn't received. And partly because, strange as it sounded, even to himself, Lucas felt that, in the end, *he'd* been the lucky one.

He had managed to escape, saving himself from his mother's grasping bitterness. In the process, he'd become a man he was proud to be. Rick, on the other hand, had been left behind to grow to manhood under the thumb of his domineering mother.

Quite simply, Lucas felt he owed him.

And now the debt wouldn't be paid until he'd brought his brother's killer to justice.

Opening the door of the Cherokee, Lucas took a moment to toss his Paisley silk tie and gray suit jacket onto the seat. Climbing in, he slammed the door, gunned the engine to life and headed out of the parking lot. The Galaxies offices would be closed by now, but as the new partner, he had a key. . . and a perfect right to forage around in his brother's computer files to see what he could find that might explain a murder.

4

DURING DINNER in the parking lot of the fast-food restaurant, Natalie changed her plans and decided to take advantage of the remaining daylight hours to do a little people-oriented investigating. Rick's office files, after all, would still be there after dark, but people were more apt to open their homes and answer questions in the daylight. Not that she had much trouble in that regard at any time. A woman was automatically viewed as less threatening than a man; and a woman as short as she was wouldn't be considered a threat even if she went knocking on doors at midnight.

Natalie grimaced into her rearview mirror as she backed out of the parking space. For the umpteenth time, she wondered whether it was a form of poetic justice or just some weird cosmic joke that her aggravating lack of stature—a trait that prevented most people from taking her as seriously as she would have liked—had turned out to be one of her prime advantages as a private investigator.

Heading her car west, she drove toward Lake Minnetonka to pay Rick and Sherri's neighbors a visit.

Unknowing tips from neighbors had provided the key to many a case for Natalie. Neighbors were the people who noticed the everyday things: a neighbor talking to a stranger; a car parked where it shouldn't be; a couple arguing out on their deck; someone carrying a large box into their house or a gas can into their garage.... All might seem to be unimportant events until the right questions were asked.

The Peytons' neighbors, however, provided zilch. Or very nearly. No suspicious-looking strangers. No odd comings-and-goings. There had been one argument out on the deck, though. Not between Rick and his perfect little wife, but between Rick and an unknown someone on the other end of a cordless telephone.

"Rick was real agitated," said Natalie's source. "Real agitated and upset, you know? He'd lost some bet. Football, I guess. It was play-off time. Anyway, he was carrying on about the spread tripping him up or something. I don't remember, exactly."

"Did he mention any names?"

"Names? You mean, like what football team he'd bet on?"

"No," Natalie said patiently. "Like who he was talking to?"

"I don't think so.... Maybe."

"Take your time." She leaned toward him, her head tilted in a way that indicated absorbed interest, her pen poised over the very official-looking clipboard in her hand. "Did he mention *any* names at all?"

"Well, I think he called the guy Mr. Rob or Bob— something like that. I don't recall exactly. I was in a hurry to get back in the house because it was damn cold outside."

"May I ask what you were doing out on your deck in ...? When was it exactly?" Natalie prodded delicately.

"December. It was the middle of December. I remember because there were Christmas lights all over. And I was outside sneaking a cigarette. I'd been trying to quit and didn't want my wife to know," the man admitted sheepishly. "Anyway, a couple of days later, I said something about it to Rick. You know, a joke because I didn't want my wife to know I was still sneaking smokes and he didn't want his to know he was betting on football. He looked at me like he didn't know what in hell I was talking about."

It wasn't much, Natalie admitted as she walked back to her car after diligently canvasing every unit within sight of the Peyton condo. It probably wasn't anything. Lots of men bet on football, lots of men lost, and most of them probably preferred that their wives not know about it.

All in all, the drive out to Lake Minnetonka had been a wasted trip, unless—

There was still plenty of daylight left, and as long as she was in the neighborhood, she decided, there was one more thing she could check out. Sliding behind the wheel of her midsize, mid-priced, medium-gray Ford sedan, Natalie reached for her car phone. Punching in her own number, she checked her messages and then, satisfied that there was nothing that couldn't be handled the next day, she dialed Information. Jotting down the number they gave her on the outside of Lucas's pil-

fered file, she quickly redialed, letting the phone ring
twenty times before concluding there was no one home.

Good, she thought with satisfaction. *Something is
finally going right*. She certainly didn't want to take a
chance on Lucas spotting her while she interviewed *his*
neighbors. Unfortunately, when she finally found the
place—after winding around thirty twisting miles of
Lake Minnetonka's one hundred and ten miles of
shoreline—there weren't any.

Neighbors, that is.

His twelve acres consisted of undeveloped, privacy-
protecting woodlands. His house was basically a log
cabin, with the additions he'd gotten all those permits
to build jutting out from the main structure at odd and
charming angles. There was a path of sorts leading up
to two long, half-timbered steps and a narrow, porti-
coed front porch with a rustic, rough-hewn railing.
Three pots of wildly overgrown red geraniums were
suspended in rope hangers along the edge of the
porch—the only attempt, as far as she could see, at any
"landscaping" beyond that provided by Mother Na-
ture.

Thwarted in her mission to interview his nonexistent neighbors, Natalie spent a good five seconds de-
bating the wisdom of doing a little judicious snooping.
On the one hand, if Lucas suddenly showed up, she'd
have no reason except the obvious one for what she was
doing at his place, not to mention that she wasn't exactly dressed for tromping through the woods. On the
other hand, the worst he could do if she did show up was
to throw her off his property.

The place didn't look especially lived-in—the drapes were drawn tightly on the windows, no dog had come bounding from around the back of the house to greet her, and the geraniums had a rather untended look about them. Perhaps he just used the place as a weekend retreat, in which case he wasn't likely to show up now.

Natalie was already out of the car by the time her reasoning took her that far, and was mincing her way up the uneven path in the half-formed hope the front door had been left unlocked. It hadn't. Undeterred, she headed around to the lake side of the house. Stepping up onto a large, multilevel cedar deck, she tried the sliding door, giving it a few hard tugs before conceding that it, too, was securely locked.

"Damn," she swore, wishing for just a moment that her father hadn't instilled in his children such a healthy respect for the law. In situations like this, it would have been helpful if her moral code didn't preclude breaking and entering.

She sighed and turned, gazing out over the placid lake, trying to decide what her next step should be. There was a narrow dock at the water's edge with a faded red-and-white-striped awning tented over what looked to be an old and meticulously maintained powerboat. She could see the sparkling reflections of sunlight off its brass fixtures from where she stood.

Without giving much thought to what she hoped to find, but hoping to find *something* to justify the long trip out here, Natalie crossed the deck and carefully picked her way down the rocky path to the lake. As she stepped onto the floating dock, she was suddenly aware of its narrowness and the way it dipped under even her slight weight. She took half a dozen cautious steps, then had to stop when the narrow heel of one of her shoes caught between the wooden planks.

"Damn!" she swore a second time. "This just isn't my day."

Carefully she bent her knee and tugged, testing to see if her shoe would come free with her foot still in it. It wouldn't—not without serious damage to the teal-blue leather. She crouched down to unbuckle the narrow ankle strap. The dock shifted. Alarmed, Natalie tried to stand, lifting her arms to regain her balance, and shifting her free foot to widen her stance. But she overcorrected and tilted forward. Unable to compensate for her trapped foot, she hovered for a second, arms flailing, body teetering, and then, with an angry squeal, she pitched, face first, into the lake. Just before she hit the water, she felt the heel of her shoe snap, sending a jolt up her leg.

LUCAS KNEW SOMEONE was at the lake house thirty seconds after Natalie's car turned into his long, winding driveway. There was a trip wire embedded across the entrance, just under the surface of the gravel road, which had sounded a discreet alarm on the specialized pager he carried with him.

He wasn't particularly worried; he was on his way home, anyway, and people sometimes turned into his driveway looking for another address or thinking it was a public road, despite the Private Drive sign he had posted. Keeping a steady foot on the gas pedal, he punched a two-number code into his pager to silence the soft, insistent buzz of the alarm, expecting any minute to hear it sound again as whoever had wandered down his driveway realized their mistake and rolled over the hidden wire on their way out.

What he heard was the slightly different signal that told him someone was at his front door. The lost traveler, he guessed, seeking directions. But the alarm sounded again a minute or two later, alerting him to the fact that whoever it was had just tried the sliders at the back of the house.

More than a lost traveler, he realized, pressing down on the Jeep's accelerator.

He came to a stop halfway down his driveway, out of sight of the house and whoever was violating his privacy. Quietly he went around to the back of the four-wheel-drive vehicle, opened the rear door and the locked gun box, and extracted a long, sleek rifle. Then, stealthily as a hunting cat, he moved off toward the house in an easy, ground-eating run, with the rifle hanging loosely at his side.

He pulled up short a moment later, seeing Natalie's two-year-old gray Ford at just about the same instant his pager sounded again, telling him someone had stepped onto his dock. He silenced the pager with an impatient stab of his forefinger. "Damned nosy little—"

There was a short, surprised shout and a splash. Lucas broke into a loping run again, rounding the corner of his log house just in time to see Natalie rise, sputtering and unsteady, from the murky green water of the lake.

Her formerly stylish blond bob streamed over her face and neck in thick, wet rattails. Rivers of water ran down her chic little blue suit, plastering the material to every alluring curve. Her glasses hung comically askew, dangling from one ear.

Lucas couldn't help the grin that spread across his face. *Serves the little sexpot right!* he thought as he snapped the rifle's safety into place. Hoisting it casually over his shoulder, he strolled the rest of the way down to the lake, prepared to thoroughly enjoy himself at his uninvited guest's expense.

Natalie floundered in the thigh-deep water, unaware she was being watched. With one hand she pushed her wet hair out of her eyes and her glasses into place. With the other, she flailed around in an effort to keep her balance as she struggled toward shore on uneven heels and a sandy lake-bottom. She stumbled twice—going under completely the first time so that only quick action kept her from losing her glasses; pitching forward into another face-first flop the second time. The water lapped harmlessly around her elbows when she caught herself on her hands and knees, so she stayed down, deciding it would be easier to crawl the rest of the way to dry land.

"That's probably the only smart thing you've done all day—" Lucas paused for effect "—little girl."

Natalie froze in midcrawl. Her head snapped up—and up—until she was staring through water-spattered glasses into the wickedly amused green eyes of the last person on earth she wanted to see just then. The four-letter word that passed her lips was wonderfully expressive of her feelings at the moment.

"Your daddy know you talk like that?"

Natalie swore again and pushed herself upright so that she could glare at him from a slightly more dignified position. It didn't improve things much from her perspective; being on her knees in front of him was only slightly better than being on all fours. Especially when he continued to stand there at the water's edge, as casual as you please, one hip thrust out and his wrists slung loosely over either end of the rifle that was resting across his broad shoulders. He made absolutely no attempt to hide the look of unholy amusement in his eyes. Even the cobra tattooed on the back of his right hand seemed to be smirking at her.

Natalie's eyes narrowed. "You could at least help me out," she said sharply, holding out her hand.

Lucas shook his head. "You got yourself in, you can get yourself out."

Natalie's hand fell back into the water at her side with unnecessary force, splashing droplets as far as the toes of his shiny calfskin shoes. "Okay, fine." She dropped sideways to her hip, swinging her feet around in front of her as she did so. Sitting in six inches of water, her skirt tucked between her thighs to keep it from floating up and exposing her all, she struggled with the wet ankle straps of her formerly beautiful teal-blue shoes. "This isn't the least bit funny, you know," she said, furious when she heard his low laugh.

"It is from where I'm standing."

She shot him a fierce glare over the tops of her spattered glasses without pausing in her efforts to separate the slippery leather straps from the tiny buckles that bound them to her ankles.

"Serves you right, you know," he said conversationally, wondering how soon she'd realize that keeping her skirt tucked between her pretty little knees didn't conceal much when those very same knees were drawn right up to her chest. "Breaking and entering is against the law."

"I do *not* indulge in breaking and entering," she retorted primly, throwing one shoe up onto the sandy soil by his feet.

The same way, he thought, *that you "do not" bat your eyelashes.*

"I came out to talk to you," she improvised, bending to her second shoe. "And when no one answered the front door I came around to see if you might be out on your boat."

"After trying the sliders."

Natalie's hand stilled. She looked up. "Says who?"

"I knew the minute you turned into the driveway. You tried the front door first, then came around the back to see if you could jimmy the sliders."

She gave him a carefully blank look, as if she had no earthly idea what he was talking about.

"I'm an expert in computer security, remember?" He slid the rifle from behind his neck and leaned it against a small boulder as he spoke. "The house is wired. So's the driveway. And the dock. If you'd stepped foot on the boat, all hell would've broken loose. It's rigged with an audible siren that can be heard halfway across the lake."

Natalie gave him her full attention then, unaware that the backs of her thighs were in full view. Or that the narrow strip of nylon fabric between her legs flickered in and out of Lucas's sight with her agitated movements and the gentle lapping of the water around her. "Are you telling me that you're responsible for my little dip?" she demanded indignantly. "That the dock is rigged to dump people?"

"Nope. That was just your own clumsiness." Unable to stand it another minute, he crouched by the water's edge. "Here, let me take a whack at that." He reached out, grabbed her ankle, and yanked her leg toward him.

The abrupt movement sent her sprawling back on her elbows. "Just what do you think you're doing?" she sputtered, trying to pull her foot out of his hand while reaching to push her skirt down.

He seemed to barely notice her struggling. "You're just making it harder on yourself—*"and me!"*—fooling with it like that." He slipped a finger under the strap, breaking it with one sharp tug.

"My shoe!" Natalie wailed.

"What are you hollering about?" He dropped her foot back into the water. "The damn thing was already broken."

"I could have gotten the heel fixed."

"Well, you can get the strap fixed, too, if you want." He stood, dropping the shoe beside its mate as he did so. "Although, personally, I don't know why you'd want to. They look like hooker shoes to me."

"Hooker shoes!"

"You know—" he leaned over and picked up his rifle "—the kind women wear with nothing but a smile in those pinup magazines?"

"I'll have you know I paid one hundred and fifty dollars for those shoes," Natalie informed him. "They're the very latest th—"

"High-class-hooker shoes, then. Come on—" he extended his free hand "—haul yourself outta there."

It would have given Natalie a great deal of satisfaction at that point to refuse his help—*hooker shoes, indeed!*—but she managed to suppress the impulse in favor of good sense. The shadows were lengthening into dusk and she was getting cold, despite the lingering heat of the summer day. Reaching up, she put her hand in his and let him haul her out of Lake Minnetonka's chilling waters.

"Ow! Wait a minute!" She hung back when he started to drag her up the path behind him.

"What's the matter now?"

"My feet are bare, in case you haven't noticed."

He looked down the length of her long, wet legs. Oh, he'd noticed all right—and then some. Lucas sighed, sounding very much like her father when she'd pushed him just a bit too far. "I suppose you want me to carry you?"

"Of course not." *I'd rather eat lutefisk for breakfast!* she thought, and she hated fish. "I have a pair of tennis shoes in my car."

"And you want me to go get them for you?"

"It would be the gentlemanly thing to do," she replied, making it sound very much as if she doubted he was entitled to that designation.

Lucas shook his head.

"Why on earth not?"

"Because I don't trust you out of my sight. That's why not."

"Well, for heaven's sake," she said, exasperated. "If I can't walk to the house, I'm certainly not going to go anywhere else."

Lucas shook his head again, refusing to see the reasonableness of her argument. He couldn't have said why he was being so perverse, except that he enjoyed needling her.

"Well, then . . ." Her chin came up to hide her sudden nervousness. "I guess you will have to carry me."

Lucas sighed again, very much the put-upon male. "This shirt is custom-made, in case you're interested."

Natalie gave him a look that said she wasn't, trying not to let her gaze wander to the shoulders that made custom tailoring necessary.

"And you're soaking wet."

"I'll have it laundered, okay?"

"Oh, hell," he muttered ungraciously, angry over the fact that he was willing to use any lame excuse to put his arms around her. "All right, come here." He motioned her with his free arm as he spoke, making it clear he expected her to drape herself over his shoulder.

"Not like that," Natalie protested, backing away.

"Then how?"

"You know." She made a motion of her own. "The regular way."

"And what am I supposed to do with my rifle?"

"You carry me. I'll carry it."

He gave her a long, slow, thorough look—from the top of her wet, bedraggled head and water-splattered glasses, over her dripping suit, down the inch-wide run in the left leg of her panty hose, to the toes of her shoeless feet. "If you think I'm handing you a gun, you're even crazier than I thought." With that, he ducked his shoulder into her midsection and stood, wrapping his arm around the backs of her knees to hold her in place.

Natalie screeched in affronted outrage. "Put me down, you caveman! You macho ape! You—" She paused for a second to rescue her slipping glasses. "—you *Marine!* Dammit—" She planted a solid thud with her clenched fist against his broad back to little visible effect. "Put me down!"

He smacked her on the bottom with the barrel of his rifle. "Shut up and hold still or I'll toss you back in the lake!"

5

HE CARRIED HER up the path and across the cedar deck with annoying ease. Transferring his rifle to the hand that anchored her legs, he unlocked the sliding-glass doors, carried her inside and, one-handedly, punched in a code on a numbered panel to disable the alarm. Her weight shifted, necessitating a quick grab at his shirt, as he leaned to set his rifle against the wall.

He snapped on a light, and Natalie found herself staring, upside down, at a planked wooden floor, a bit of bright hooked rug and a very shapely pair of male buns covered in conservative gray gabardine speckled with water drops. It made her dizzy. "You can put me down now," she said as sweetly as she could, not wanting to risk another whack across the fanny.

"In a minute." Her weight shifted again as he turned to maneuver her through another door and down a short, carpeted hallway. "I don't want you dripping all over the floor."

"I'm going to drip whether you put me down or—"

He leaned forward slightly as he stepped through a third door, and let her slide down his body. It was a long slide that allowed his big hand to glide up the backs of her thighs and her bottom and the sensitive small of her back as he guided her to her feet.

"—not," she finished breathlessly. Her feet were between his. Her hands were resting lightly on his powerful biceps. Her eyes were on a level with the acres of soft custom-tailored cotton covering his chest; it was wet where she had lain against it, and clung to every awesome curve of muscle and the hard little button of his nipple.

Was it hard from the cold and wet? she wondered. Or in response to the same heat that was suddenly gripping her?

Her hands tightened for a moment, as if to bring him closer in their almost-embrace, and then flattened as if to keep him from moving that scant inch or two that would make the embrace overwhelmingly real.

But he was already drawing back of his own accord, making any further action on her part unnecessary. "There are plenty of towels in the cabinet, there," he said abruptly, annoyed with himself for having so little control over his reactions to her. "Go ahead and take a hot shower if you want." *I, on the other hand, could use a cold one!* "Just wring your clothes out and toss them outside the door." He was backing out of the small bathroom as he spoke. "I'll throw 'em in the dryer."

"That won't be necessary," Natalie quickly replied. No way did she want to risk being naked in the same house with this man. "I'll just blot off the worst of it and it'll be fine. Really." She followed her words with action, grabbing a towel off the rack to dab at her clothes. "I'll have to borrow one of these to sit on for the drive home, but—"

"No."

"No?" Natalie looked up at him. "No, what? You don't want me borrowing one of your towels?"

"No, I don't want you leaving yet," he clarified.

Natalie felt her pulse flutter. "And just what is that supposed to mean?" she demanded, denying the flutter was anything other than annoyance at his presumption in issuing what amounted to an order.

"Just what it sounded like. You're not leaving until I say you can leave."

The flutter became a pounding. "If you think you can keep me here against my will, buster," she countered, drawing herself up to her full height, "you have another think coming."

"And if you think I actually *want* you here, against your will or not, you've got a screw loose. But you're the one who invited yourself out here and you're not leaving until you answer a few questions."

"I don't have to take my clothes off to answer a few questions," she said, and then clamped her mouth shut.

Lucas's hand tightened on the doorknob. "You don't have to take your clothes off at all. You can stand around for however long it takes in that soggy suit and turn as blue as it is, for all I care. I, however, am going to change into something more comfortable. And you can wipe that crafty look right off your face, little girl, because I've already taken the keys out of your car."

"Don't call me little girl!" she exclaimed furiously as the door slammed shut. "I hate to be called little girl," she muttered.

"There's a robe on the back of the door if you decide to be sensible," Lucas said through the wooden panel.

"But whatever you decide, get it done in ten minutes because that's all the time I'm giving you." Then he hotfooted it out to the car to do what he said he'd already done.

Natalie stuck her tongue out at the plaid flannel robe hanging on the bathroom door and decided to be reasonable—on *her* timetable.

Twenty minutes later, warmed from the shower, her hair slicked back and her glasses wiped clean, wrapped from neck to fingertips and floor in soft red-plaid flannel, Natalie opened the bathroom door. Taking a deep breath to ready herself for battle, she gathered up the folds of the robe and padded down the hallway and into the living room.

Lucas looked up from the file he was reading. "You've been busy."

"Just doing my job," Natalie replied, deciding to brazen it out. "Everything in that file is a matter of public record." She made her way across the smooth wooden floor and onto the colorful oval of the hooked rug, to an old bentwood rocker. It was as far away from the corner of the sofa where Lucas sat reading his file as the room arrangement would allow. "Anyone in the world could get the same information just by asking."

"But not everyone is nosy enough to ask."

"Not everyone is a private investigator," she said with a pardonable touch of pride.

"A paid snoop, you mean."

"I *said* what I meant," she answered crisply, stung by his careless disregard for her chosen profession; it was uncomfortably close to her father's opinion. "It's a perfectly legitimate profession."

His answer was a disagreeable snort and a view of the top of his head as he flipped to the second page of her notes and resumed reading.

Natalie bent her knees, bringing her bare feet onto the seat of the chair, and tucked the robe down over her toes. There was nothing to do now but wait him out. Well, she was good at that. Stationary surveillance wasn't exactly her favorite part of the job at any time, but it usually proved to be useful. She put her considerable powers of observation to work on her jailer first, on the theory that the more you know about your enemy, the better it was for you.

He'd changed clothes, switching from his proper businessman's disguise—not that he'd looked the least bit proper in it, anyway—to old gray sweats and a faded olive-green T-shirt that was probably a relic of his Marine past. It clung to the broad shoulders and impressive chest muscles, stretching to tautness over the smooth mounds of his powerful biceps.

Natalie gulped and looked away, searching for something to focus her attention on other than the man who would, no doubt, try to use it to his advantage if he knew how much he turned her on.

He obviously liked old things—the bentwood rocker, the pair of nineteenth-century taboret tables in front of the sofa, the painted wooden carving of an American bald eagle with its wings outspread over the half-timbered mantel of the fieldstone fireplace. He liked comfort—the cushy sofa and big upholstered chairs, the well-placed lights, the hooked rug beneath his bare feet. He liked practicality—the easy-care wooden floor, the rugged sailcloth covering the sofa and chairs; the huge, screened, double-paned windows that were now open to the lake breezes—he must have done that while she was in the bathroom—or closed tight against fierce winter winds blowing across frozen water.

She spent a moment wishing she didn't agree with his likes quite so much, then distracted herself by wondering where all the computer equipment was. The only other computer fanatic she knew intimately—*personally*, she amended hurriedly; no way did she intend to ever know Lucas Sinclair intimately!—was Daniel, and his apartment looked like an electronics store.

Lucas's place looked as if he'd never heard the word *computer.*

He finished reading and looked up, catching her unawares as she surveyed his surroundings. She suited the name he'd taunted her with, looking little-girl fragile with her knees tucked up under her chin and her toes covered by the trailing hem of his robe. He just wished to hell he could stop fantasizing about all the bare, womanly flesh hidden beneath the enveloping garment.

He knew she had more than her fair share of curves, considering how small she was. He'd seen her—breasts, waist and hips, all lush and feminine—outlined by the soaking-wet blue suit. He'd felt her—every soft, giving curve—sliding slowly down his body when he lowered her to her feet. For one brief moment, there, he'd been sorely tempted to pick her up again and carry her off to his bed. He had a feeling she wouldn't have protested much.

There was something in her eyes, something in the way she challenged him in a purely woman-to-man way, that told him she was as attracted to him as he was to her. Something, too, that let him know she didn't like that particular little twist of fate one bit more than he did. She apparently knew as well as he did that they were opposites who should stay as far away from each other as possible, no matter how physically attracted they were.

And it *was* simply physical, he assured himself; she wasn't his type at all.

He was determined to ignore what wasn't good for him and get on with the business at hand. "Just find out who murdered Rick," he muttered.

"Beg pardon?"

Natalie was staring at him as if he might do something dangerous at any moment.

"Nothing," he mumbled, annoyed at having been caught talking to himself. He nodded toward the mug on the little drum table in front of him. "Would you like a cup of coffee before we get started?"

"Before the interrogation begins, you mean?"

"If that's how you want to think of it."

"I prefer not to think of it at all," she told him. "And, yes, I'd like a cup of coffee. I was wondering when you were going to offer one," she added, just to let him know she hadn't overlooked his lapse in manners.

"Kitchen's through that door," he directed with a jerk of his thumb. "Coffee's on the stove."

Natalie didn't move.

"What's the matter now?"

"It's normally considered polite for a host to serve his guests."

"You're not a guest, you're a trespasser. And I don't go out of my way to be polite to trespassers. Or women's libbers," he added, just to get her hackles up. "You modern ladies—excuse me—women," he corrected with exaggerated politeness. "You modern women are always complaining about how all the outdated rituals of civilized society are keeping you from being treated as equals." His voice was tinged with a bitterness that revealed more than he intended. "Well, I'm treating you like an equal. Feel free to help yourself."

Natalie got up without another word and, gathering the folds of his robe around her, headed for the kitchen. *Well, my, my,* she thought as she found a mug and poured herself a steaming cup of coffee. *His wife really must have done a number on him. His wife and,* she amended, *his witch of a mother.* No wonder he had all the characteristics of a house cat gone feral. Perhaps a change of tactics was in order, she mused, tapping her finger against the edge of the coffee mug.

But first she had to know something.

"Do you mind if I use your phone?" she hollered from the kitchen. "It's a local call."

"Calling for help won't do you any good." Lucas's voice was nearer than she expected. Startled, she turned just in time to see him saunter into the kitchen, mug in hand. "I could have you begging to tell me everything you know before anyone could get out here to save you," he said casually, reaching for the coffeepot.

Natalie raised an eyebrow, unimpressed by his efforts to intimidate. "A little something they taught you in the Marines?"

He flashed her an evil smile over the rim of his coffee mug. "Among other things." Motioning toward the phone with his mug, he said, "Be my guest. Call anyone you want, if it will make you feel better."

Natalie lifted the receiver off its cradle, then paused, looking over at him where he lounged with his hip against the kitchen counter. "Do you mind?" she demanded tartly. "This is a private call."

Lucas shrugged and sauntered back into the main room.

Watching to make sure he was actually leaving—and to admire the flex of his really rather spectacular rear end under the soft fleece of his sweatpants—Natalie quickly punched in her father's number.

"Hi, Dad, it's me," she said without preamble. "No, I haven't forgiven you yet, but I might if you'll answer a couple of questions for me. Yes—" the word was drawn out and exasperated "—about Lucas Sinclair."

"Shoot," replied her father.

Natalie lowered her voice, hunching a shoulder toward the wall for even more privacy. "What did he want to talk to you about this afternoon?"

"Same thing I wanted to talk to him about. His half brother's murder."

"I know that. I mean specifically."

"Specifically? Well, specifically, he wanted to see the medical report. And the lab report from the guys who went over the car. He wanted to know if we had any solid leads or suspects. Or any hope in hell of having either in the foreseeable future. All the usual who, what, where and why any next-of-kin wants to know." He paused. "Not that it's any of your business."

Natalie ignored that. "Did you tell him?"

"Of course, I told him. Why wouldn't I have told him?"

Natalie took a deep breath and hunched her shoulder even more. "Then you don't think he had anything to do with Rick's murder?"

"Hell, no."

"Why not?"

"Gut instinct, that's why not. Plus the fact that he wasn't even in town when it happened. He was out in L.A. last week, installing one of those high-tech monster security systems in some paranoid rock star's mansion. Just got back the day after Rick was killed. He gave me the guy's number in case I wanted to call and check his story."

"Did you?"

"What do you think, little girl?"

"You did."

"Damn straight. And it checked out. This rock star's secretary was real impressed with our boy, too. Melted like a snow cone at the state fair when I mentioned his name."

Natalie tried to convince herself she hadn't experienced a similar reaction. "Some women are easily impressed," she said dryly.

Nathan chuckled. "The secretary was a guy."

"Goodbye, Dad." She hung up without giving him a chance to enjoy his little joke, then stood for a moment with her hand on the receiver, thinking things through. A decision made, she picked up her coffee mug and went back into the living room to convince Lucas to go along with it.

She sat on the sofa this time, not too close to Lucas, but not in the opposite corner, either. Her feet flat on the hooked rug, knees together, she took a bracing sip of caffeine. "Well," she said, looking at him from over the rim of her mug, "where do we begin?"

From the look on his face, it was evident he hadn't expected quite so direct an approach.

Natalie smiled behind her coffee mug; she'd show him how a *really* liberated woman operated; it would do him a world of good. Not to mention making things a little safer for the next "modern" woman he encountered.

"Are you going to ask me questions, or should I just tell you what I've learned up to this point?" she asked.

Lucas indicated the file he still held. "I know what you've learned." He dropped it on the sofa between them and reached for his coffee. "And none of it is exactly news to me."

"Not everything is in that file," she informed him. "I haven't had time to write it all down."

"And you're willing to tell me what you didn't write down?"

"Uh-hmm."

Lucas leaned forward, his elbows on his knees, his mug cradled between his palms, his gaze cynical and speculative as he assessed her.

Natalie sat up a bit straighter, doing her best to look cooperative.

"All right, Natalie." He leaned back in the corner of the sofa with the mug in his hand. "What are you up to?"

"Up to?" she echoed, aware that it was the first time he'd called her by name, and trying not to dwell on how nice it sounded, coming from him.

"When a woman gets all round-eyed and innocent, it's a sure sign she's up to something."

"Well, you're wrong. I'm not up to anything. I just thought, well, since we're both working on the same case, so to speak, we could—" she shrugged casually, looking at him out of the corner of her eye to see how he was taking it "—work together."

"Since when are we working on the same case? I thought I was your main suspect."

"You were never my main suspect. Just my only one. And I've had time to reconsider."

"When? Between now and the time you went into the kitchen?" There was a beat of silence not nearly long enough for her to answer his question. "You called your father," he stated.

"Yes."

"And he told you I was innocent."

"Hardly innocent," Natalie corrected, unable to pass up such a perfect opening. "But certainly not involved in your brother's murder."

"Well, thank you, Ms. Bishop, for that vote of confidence."

"Oh, for heaven's sake! There's no need to get all huffy. Who was a more logical choice as a suspect? You were the one who benefited most from Rick's death," she pointed out. "You were also an unknown quantity. And you do have specialized training," she added craftily, hoping she could get him to reveal what he'd done with the U.S. government that was so secret.

"Training?" he questioned mildly.

"Military intelligence."

"I was in cryptographics."

"So you say."

He gave her a look of condescending amusement. "You've seen too many James Bond movies. Military intelligence doesn't always mean espionage and dark alleys. It also means secretaries and file clerks and—"

"Cryptographers. Yes, I'm sure it does. But you didn't get that nose sitting in front of a computer."

"I got it in a sleazy bar in Texas, right after boot camp." And he had. The first time, anyway, when he was still into brawling.

"And you didn't learn to handle a rifle as if it were an extension of your arm from a computer, either," she insisted stubbornly, determined to make him fit her image of him.

"For God's sake, Natalie! I was a Marine. They teach all of us to use guns. If they didn't, I'd never have survived two tours in Nam."

"Maybe, but—"

"Your problem is you're letting my mother's glowing accolades influence you too much." His pale green gaze locked with hers. "I haven't been that stupid hell-raising kid since my first action in Nam."

"Yes, well . . ." She fidgeted in uneasy silence for a moment, wondering if what he'd said just might be true. Nothing she'd found in his records at the county courthouse indicated he'd kept up the activities that had landed him in so much trouble as a kid. Maybe he *had* changed.

And maybe pigs could fly.

"Why don't you tell me why you were snooping around my place?" Lucas said into the silence.

"I wasn't snoop— All right, I was," she admitted when he gave her a look she was sure had caused many a battle-hardened Marine to tremble in his combat boots. "But not because of what your mother said."

"No?"

"No," she stated, so emphatically he believed her. "I wanted to check you out because you're Daniel's new partner and none of us know anything about you."

He tapped the file that lay on the sofa beside him. "So you invaded my privacy."

"Like I said, there's nothing in there that isn't a matter of public record."

"Maybe. But that still doesn't tell me why you came out here. This place isn't public anything, in case you hadn't noticed."

"Look, I admit I came out here with the idea of conducting a little survey on you, okay? I was going to talk to your neighbors, see what I could come up with. And, then, when I got out here and there weren't any neighbors, well, I wasn't crazy about having driven all this way for nothing, so I decided to have a look around is all. No harm in that, is there?"

"None at all," he agreed dryly.

"So ... Are we partners?"

"What's in it for me?"

"The services of an experienced private investigator."

"The police are giving me that," he reminded her.

"While they investigate two dozen other cases at the same time," she shot back. "We could devote more time and attention to this than the police ever could. Come on, Lucas, I know you're not crazy about 'modern' women," she said earnestly when he failed to agree. "And I'm sure it won't come as a surprise to you that I haven't exactly got a soft spot—" *not much of one, anyway*"—for swaggering, two-fisted ex-Marines with sexist chips on their shoulders, but I think we can work together."

He grunted. "Go on."

She edged closer to him, reaching over to set her coffee mug on the little drum table. "Okay, this is the way I see our partnership working. I'm the investigator. I've already talked to all of Rick and Sherri's neighbors. I didn't get much." She waved her hand. "But that doesn't matter. I plan to start questioning the other businesses in the office park tomorrow and, sooner or later, I'll find *something*. All it takes is one small lead— one clue to start me in the right direction."

"And where do I fit in this, ah, partnership?" he asked, dividing his attention between her glowing, eager face and the red plaid fabric that had parted over her legs to reveal her rounded knees and most of one sleek thigh.

"You're the computer whiz," she said, as if his part should be crystal clear. "You go through Rick's computer files and see what you can dig up. I was going to do that myself, but, well, if you want the truth—"

"By all means, let's have the truth."

"I'm not much good with machines," she confessed, ignoring his sarcasm. "Daniel got all the computer genes in our family, I guess. Anyway—" She brushed that fact aside as being of no importance and leaned in even closer, giving him the full benefit of her eager, wide-eyed gaze and, unwittingly, the widening gap in the lapels of his robe. "What do you say?"

Lucas didn't know what the hell to say. Did he really want to be partners with a pushy little sexpot? Did he want to work side by side with the kind of "modern" woman he'd learned the hard way to avoid? It would probably be one of the stupidest things he'd done in his life, ranking right up there with getting roaring drunk the day he'd become a Marine and ending up with a cobra tattooed around his wrist. But, yes, dammit, he wanted to be her partner—her bed partner!

Natalie seemed to sense his imminent capitulation. She offered her hand. "Partners?"

Lucas hesitated for a heartbeat, then sighed and gave in to the inevitable. Reaching out, he set his coffee mug on the taboret table in front of him. "Partners," he agreed, taking her much smaller, softer hand in his. Then, without giving himself time to think better of it, he reached out with his other hand and removed her glasses.

"Wha—?" Natalie began, but it was too late.

Before the word was even out of her mouth, he'd pulled her into his arms and planted his lips solidly over hers.

Natalie's first response was to flatten her palms against his chest as if to push him away. Her second and much stronger response was to press closer and give him more of what he'd already taken. She went with her second response. Letting her head fall back, she opened her mouth to his seeking tongue, pressing her flannel-covered breasts to the hard wall of his chest. He leaned into her with a ragged groan, pushing her down into the corner of the cushy sofa with the weight of his power-ful body. She went with that, too—encouraged it, even, blindly sliding her hands up over his wide shoulders as if to guide him down on top of her. The kiss deepened and his mouth angled over hers as their lips ate at each other's, and their tongues engaged in a heated pas de deux.

Natalie felt herself softening, curling into the strong arms that held her, losing herself in that age-old femi-nine response to the welcome passion of an aggressive, aroused man. Every avowed feminist principle she professed to hold dear—not to mention a well-developed instinct for self-preservation—should have been screaming in alarmed protest. But, Lord, she loved the feel of him—his heat and hardness, his *maleness*. The way he towered over her, surrounded her, enveloped her in a cocoon of warmth and passion made her feel defenceless and protected and strangely powerful—all at the same time.

She moaned softly in both protest and acceptance, then tore her mouth from his. "I shouldn't," she whispered, knowing it was true. Even if he hadn't been exactly the type of man she'd sworn to avoid like the plague, it would have been true. She hardly knew him. And she never got this intimate this quickly with a man she hardly knew. "Lucas, we really shouldn't."

"I know," Lucas said raggedly. His mouth went on a fevered journey across her cheek and jaw and down the arched column of her throat. "But, Lord, I want you." He bit softly into the tender place where her neck curved into her shoulder.

Natalie stiffened again, this time in sheer delight, then melted into a languorous, mind-drugging excitement. *He bit me!* she thought, a little aghast at herself for being aroused by so primitive a sign of his desire. It sent shivers down her spine and bolts of exquisite heat to her most feminine parts.

"I've wanted you since the first time I laid eyes on you," he growled into her ear.

"You have?" she murmured, impossibly pleased that her instant attraction had been returned. "Really?"

"Umm." He nuzzled aside the lapel of the robe she wore to feast on the soft skin of her shoulder. "I didn't even like you, but I wanted you, anyway."

A tiny portion of her brain began to clear. "Didn't like me?"

"Didn't think you were my type," he murmured into her neck. "But, oh, baby, are you ever my type."

"Didn't like me?" she repeated.

"I like you now," he assured her earnestly. Through the fog of his rapidly escalating passion, he sensed her withdrawal. "I like you a lot. A whole lot."

"But—"

"Don't talk." His hand slipped inside the loosened panels of the robe and closed gently over her breast.

Natalie gasped at the sizzling warmth of his large palm, strangely excited by the thought that the hand cupping her so tenderly was the same hand that bore the likeness of a coiled cobra.

"That's it, baby," he encouraged. "Don't talk, just feel." He stroked her nipple lightly with his thumb.

"Lucas . . ." She didn't know, just then, whether she spoke in entreaty or denial.

Nor did Lucas. But he wasn't taking any chances. He rolled her nipple between his thumb and forefinger— liking the way it responded instantly to his touch; loving the way it made him feel to touch it; loving, too, the way her body arched beneath him as if begging for more. "Kiss me," he demanded roughly and took her mouth with his.

Natalie couldn't help herself; she kissed him—kissed him long and hard and hungrily, until her arms were locked around his neck and the red plaid robe was completely open over her breasts and one bare leg was flexed, ever so slightly, rubbing the inside of her thigh against the outside of his.

Without releasing her lips, Lucas slid his hand down her side, pushing the robe out of the way as he skimmed her bare hip, and curved his fingers around the back of her thigh. He pulled it up, high, so that her knee was above the level of his hip, shifting his own body until they were suddenly man to woman at the most basic level, with only a layer of faded gray sweatshirt fabric preventing ultimate consummation.

Natalie whimpered in anguished delight. "Oh, no. No." In a last-ditch effort to save herself, she tore her mouth from his and pushed at his shoulders. "No more."

Lost in passion, Lucas tried to recapture her mouth, pressing his erection against the sensitive cleft between the tops of her thighs as he did so.

"No more," she repeated, pushing harder. "Lucas, stop it!"

Lucas stopped, but he didn't move. "Why?" he asked in a deadly calm voice.

If she'd been thinking clearly she might have been frightened by his calm, but her mind was befuddled by frustrated passion and hurt feelings. "Because we don't like each other, that's why," she replied, giving him another, harder shove. *He* didn't like *her*, at any rate; but there was no way in hell she was going to let him know how one-sided the feeling was. "Now, get off me."

Lucas raised himself far enough to look down at her. "That was a hell of a demonstration of dislike you just gave," he growled, his eyes on her puckered nipples.

Natalie snatched the front of the robe together and scrambled to a sitting position in the corner of the sofa. "It was an aberration." She overlapped the lapels as far as they would go, and yanked the belt into a tight knot to keep them that way. "We both lost our heads for a minute, is all."

"Yeah, well . . ." Lucas flopped back into the opposite corner of the sofa, grabbing an oversize cushion to cradle over his lap, and shot her a disgruntled glare from under lowered eyebrows. "I wish yours had stayed lost for about ten minutes more."

I'll just bet you do, she thought. *Well, dammit, so do I!* "You'll get over it," she said instead, looking around for her glasses. She found them on the taboret table in front of her and slipped them on. "It isn't as if you really wanted me, anyway."

He made as if to lift the cushion. "Would you like to take a look at how much I really didn't want you?"

"There's no need to be crude."

"Oh, so now I'm crude! You didn't think I was so crude a minute ago."

"I wasn't thinking at all, a minute ago," she retorted. "And neither were you."

He wrapped his long arms around the cushion in his lap and rested his chin on it, mulishly refusing to respond to her charge.

Natalie stood. There was obviously no reasoning with him in this mood. Not that she felt particularly reasonable herself at the moment. What she really wanted to do was hit him over the head with something—preferably something breakable that would make a loud, satisfying crash when it knocked him out cold. "I think I'd better leave," she said quietly.

"Yeah," Lucas agreed, still refusing to look at her. He was feeling misled, mistreated, and miserably, achingly frustrated. Childishly he wanted her to feel the same way. "Maybe you'd better."

There was a long silence.

"I don't know where my clothes are," she reminded in a small, dignified voice.

"The laundry room is off the kitchen."

Natalie gathered up the hem of the robe, holding it aside so it wouldn't brush his legs as she moved past him. It did anyway. He looked up. Something about the unnatural stiffness of her shoulders, the proud yet vulnerable angle of her tousled head, the way his robe seemed to overpower her tiny figure as he'd tried to overpower her a moment ago, made him feel like a world-class jerk.

"Wait . . . Natalie."

She kept moving, refusing to even glance at him.

"Dammit. Natalie!" He reached out and grabbed a fistful of robe to keep her from going any farther. "I'm sorry. I'm acting like an ass," he said to her back. "Pouting like some kid who's just had his toy taken away."

Oh, great. First, he doesn't like me. Now I'm a toy!

"You had a perfect right to say no."

Well, thank you so much!

"It's just…I wish you'd said it sooner, is all. It's hard on a guy. No pun intended, I swear!" he said earnestly, when she half turned to stare at him with an incredulous look on her face. "What I mean is, well—"

"I know what you mean, Lucas." She turned to face him fully, pulling the robe out of his hand as she did so. "I may look like a little girl to you, but I'm—"

"I never said that. Well, I said it, but I didn't mean it like that. You're a beautiful, sexy woman and I—"

"But I assure you," she continued, cutting across his explanation, "I'm fully adult. I know you had your…expectations raised, so to speak, and you're feeling frustrated and angry. Well, I'm sorry about that. And if it's any consolation to you, I'm feeling pretty frustrated myself, right now. No." She backed away as he made a move to rise from the sofa. "That wasn't an invitation to start over, Lucas." She lifted her hand, palm out, to further ward him off. "So you just stay where you are."

"Natalie, I—"

"There's nothing you can say that will change my mind, so save us both the embarrassment and don't even try, okay?"

He sank back down onto the sofa without a word.

"It's much better this way," she assured him, trying to believe it herself. "We're supposed to be working on a case together, remember? A very important case. Sex would just have gotten in the way and confused the issue."

As if, he thought, *it hasn't already!*

"And, as we already agreed, I'm not your type and you're certainly not mine."

"It sure as hell felt like somebody was someone's type a minute ago," he countered, feeling compelled to point it out.

"Yes, well . . . That was just, ah, proximity and circumstances and our, ah—" she fingered the lapels of the robe, making sure they were still securely overlapped "—relative state of undress. It had nothing to do with how we really feel about each other," she lied. "So let's just save ourselves the hassle and forget it ever happened. Okay?"

Like hell I'll forget! he thought savagely. Not that she wasn't absolutely, one hundred percent right. They'd save themselves a busload of trouble if they just forgot it. She wasn't really his type, despite the luscious packaging. He just as obviously wasn't hers, no matter how heatedly she'd responded. So, okay, he'd forget it. If the ache in his groin would let him.

"Lucas?" she prompted. "Okay?"

"Okay," he mumbled.

"You don't sound too sure."

"I said okay, didn't I? I meant okay."

"All right," she responded indignantly. "There's no need to bite my head off."

"Sorry."

They stared at each other for a few seconds more, neither of them knowing quite what to say.

"Well," Natalie said stiffly, "now that that's all settled, I guess I'll just get my things and be on my way."

Lucas nodded. "Fine." He pushed himself up off the sofa, eager for any kind of action that might relieve the tension coiled in his body. "I'll go out to the car and get those tennis shoes."

"Thank you. I'd appreciate that." Natalie watched Lucas as he moved toward the front door. "They're in the trunk."

But they weren't.

"I'm sure they're there, Lucas," Natalie insisted fretfully, standing barefoot on the front porch in her badly wrinkled, slightly damp and formerly chic teal-blue suit as he searched her car a second time. "Did you check the back seat, too?"

"And under the front seat and between the seats. No sneakers."

"I don't suppose my heels . . . ?"

"Your heels have either floated away or been carried off by some curious raccoon by now."

"Oh, well." She started down the stairs toward the open door of her car, fully prepared to walk over hot coals before she'd let him carry her again. It was too dangerous for them to get that close. "I'll just have to watch my step, won't I?" she remarked, trying not to wince as her bare feet met the gravel-covered walk.

Lucas caught her up in his arms before she'd taken more than two steps. "Don't be an idiot," he growled. "It's too damn dark for you to 'watch your step,' and I'm not such a beast that I'm going to ravage you in the front seat of your car." He plopped her behind the wheel and slammed the door, leaning down with a hand on the roof to deliver his parting shot. "Not unless you ask me real nice, that is."

Natalie gave him her narrowest glare and her sweetest smile. "In your dreams, Sinclair," she retorted fiercely.

6

NATALIE ARRIVED at the suburban office-park that housed the Galaxies offices bright and early the next morning. But not early enough to avoid Lucas Sinclair, she realized as she pulled into a parking space. His black four-wheel-drive monster machine was already parked squarely in front of the doors to the Galaxies suite.

"Great," she muttered. "Just great."

It wasn't bad enough that she'd spent a thoroughly miserable night alternately dreaming hotly erotic dreams that always ended before consummation and lying awake cursing the man who'd featured prominently in every blasted one of them. It wasn't bad enough that she'd had to leave the house without so much as a cup of coffee, because she'd been in no condition to be seen shopping for groceries at the corner store last night. Apparently things weren't going to be bad enough to satisfy the powers-that-be until she'd faced Lucas Sinclair on an empty stomach.

Well, so be it. She could handle anything he threw her way and then some, she told herself, nodding confidently at the reflection that walked toward her as she approached the double glass doors to the low, sprawling building.

She'd dressed for battle in a favorite bright red suit with a slim, knee-length skirt and wide-shouldered, loosely cut jacket. The sleeveless shell underneath was a geometric print in crisp beige-and-tomato-red faux linen. Her high-heeled pumps matched the suit. Her shiny straw tote matched the beige in her blouse. The only accessories were simple but elegant gold hoop earrings and a slim gold wristwatch.

She looked feminine and classy, confident and competent—the epitome of a modern, nineties woman.

Take that, Lucas Sinclair! she thought as she pulled open the front door and stepped into the air-conditioned comfort of her brother's small suite of offices.

She stopped short at the sight of Sherri Peyton sitting behind the secretary's desk, busily sorting through a stack of what appeared to be invoices. She looked up when the door opened. "Oh, hello," she said softly and smiled her genuinely sweet smile. "It's you. I was hoping it might be Jana." Jana was the part-time secretary whose desk she occupied.

"Hello yourself," Natalie said warmly, approaching the desk. As much as the other woman annoyed her, she always felt compelled to speak gently to Sherri Peyton, now more than ever. "I don't know if today is one of Jana's days to work or not, but even if it is, she probably won't be in for another—" she glanced at her watch "—forty-five minutes, at least." She smiled at Sherri. "Which leads me to wonder what you're doing here so early."

Actually, she wondered why she was here at all. It was maybe the third time she'd ever seen Sherri in the Galaxies offices, and on the other two occasions she had stopped by to have lunch with her husband. "I kind of expected you to be spending your time at home for a while."

"So did I, but Lucas suggested I might feel better if I had something to do besides sit around and think about . . . things," she said. "He thought I might like to come down here and do something to help find out who . . . who . . ." Her bottom lip started to tremble.

"Well," Natalie said quickly, trying to forestall the tears she could see coming, "doing something always makes *me* feel better." She deposited her purse on a corner of the desk and moved toward the coffeemaker on top of the file cabinet. "Can I get you a cup?"

"No." Sherri sniffled once, deliberately, and brought herself under control. "No, I have some rose-hip tea here. Thank you, anyway."

Natalie shuddered at the thought of consuming rose hips at any time, let alone so early in the morning, and poured herself a cup of coffee. "So..." She turned with the cup in her hand. "Where is everybody?" she asked, meaning, of course, Lucas.

"I don't know where Daniel is," Sherri replied, picking up an invoice from the pile in front of her. "He hasn't come in yet. Lucas left a few minutes ago. I don't know where he is, but he said he'd be right back."

He couldn't have gone far, Natalie thought, because his Jeep was still parked outside. She wondered if that was good or bad and why she even cared. Then, pushing other considerations aside, she decided to take advantage of his absence by asking a few questions while the coast was clear. She had a sneaking suspicion Lucas wouldn't take kindly to her "pumping" his brother's sweet little widow, especially for information about him. Very casually, she propped a hip on the edge of the desk and blew on her coffee. "I didn't see your car outside. Did Lucas bring you in to the office?"

"Mm-hmm." Sherri put the invoice she was holding on one pile, then picked it up and placed it in another. "He came by early this morning—said he saw the lights on and knew I must be up."

That would make it very early indeed, thought Natalie.

"I haven't been sleeping well," Sherri confessed. "It just seems so strange to go to bed all by myself. Which is kind of funny, really," she said musingly, her hands becoming still for a moment, "because I always slept alone before I married Ricky. But it's . . . I don't know." She shook herself slightly and resumed her task. "It's just different now, I guess."

Natalie waited a moment, but when Sherri didn't go on, she prompted, "What did Lucas want?"

Sherri was studying the next invoice, her smooth forehead puckered in a frown. "When?"

Natalie took another sip of her coffee and prayed for patience. "When he stopped by your place this morning."

"Oh. He wanted to ask me some questions about the business. I'm afraid I wasn't any help, though. I've always been kind of stupid about things like that—bills and things—so Ricky took care of everything. Anyway, after breakfast, Lucas insisted on packing up Ricky's business stuff and bringing it down here—"

What will Barbara say to that? Natalie wondered.

"—that way, he'll be able to find whatever he needs without having to come out to the house all the time. Not," she said wistfully, "that I'd mind him coming out. The house seems so empty now. But Lucas said he works all hours, sometimes around the clock, and he didn't want to bother me." She looked up at Natalie. "He's really very sweet and considerate, don't you think? Not at all like Barbara said."

Natalie made a noncommittal sound and set her coffee down on the desk. "You and Lucas had breakfast together?" she asked, zeroing in on what she considered the most interesting portion of Sherri's rambling explanation.

"Uh-hmm. He wanted to take me out to eat, but I haven't really felt much like eating lately, either, not since...since the accident," she said softly. "When I told him that, well, Lucas got all big-brotherly and insisted I had to put something in my stomach, even if it was just a piece of toast. He said if I didn't want to go out and get it, I could just sit down and he'd fix it for me. But men are so useless in the kitchen." She smiled slightly, as if the thought pleased her. "And a man really needs more than toast and coffee for breakfast, which I could see right away was about all Lucas could manage without burning the place down. I made him sit at the table while I fixed him some pancakes and sausage. Pancakes were Ricky's favorite. I used to cook them for him ev—" She broke off abruptly and dropped her head into her hands with a sudden, heart-wrenching sob. "Oh, God, I miss him!"

Natalie reached out and touched her shoulder lightly, wanting to offer comfort, but not sure how to go about it. "Sherri, I—"

Sherri jumped to her feet. "Excuse me, please. I have to—" Another sob escaped her. "I need to be alone for a minute." She brushed past Natalie, rushing toward the ladies' room, the full skirt of her light summer dress flaring around her calves as she ran.

Natalie stood staring after her, feeling helpless, wondering if she should go after her or let her cry it out alone.

"What do you plan to do for your next act?" Lucas asked from the doorway. "Torture small children?"

Natalie turned, guilty and aghast at what she'd inadvertently done. "I wasn't trying to make her cry, for heaven's sake! We were talking and she just . . . fell apart."

"Maybe you should try thinking before you speak," Lucas said in a low, accusing voice. "She's in a very fragile state right now, and the slightest thing can start her crumbling."

Natalie flared instantly, thankful to have a focus for the uncharted and unchanneled emotions of the moment. "Maybe *you* should have thought about that before you dragged her down here and put her to work," she retorted, her voice equally low and no less furious than his had been. She gestured toward the invoices spread over the secretary's desk. "Handing her a stack of paperwork and taking off doesn't seem like the latest in grief therapy to me."

"Something to keep her busy is exactly what she needs right now. And I didn't 'take off.'" He advanced toward her until they were standing less than a foot apart. "I saw a guy pull up in front of the next office and decided to ask him a few casual questions about what he might have seen going on around here."

Natalie snorted inelegantly, refusing to be intimidated by his greater physical stature. "I can just picture your idea of a 'casual' question." She took a step closer and glared at him. "You probably rolled over him like a Sherman tank."

"A technique I learned from watching you in action."

"You haven't seen me in action yet, buster."

"If what I've seen so far is anything to go by, I can—"

"I'm sorry I lost control like that, Nat—" Sherri rounded the corner into the reception area and paused uncertainly. "Lucas. You're back." She glanced from one to the other of them, obviously puzzled by what she saw. Neither had altered their stance, except to turn their heads toward her, and they stood nearly toe to toe, like two combatants in the ring ready to lay into each other at the first sound of the bell. The air between them seemed to crackle with dangerous and highly volatile emotions.

"Is anything wrong?"

"No. No, of course not," they said in unison, backing away from each other as if they'd been caught in a heated embrace.

"We were just discussing our, ah—" Natalie hesitated, suddenly uncertain as to exactly what they *had* been discussing so vehemently.

"Partnership," Lucas supplied smoothly. "We were discussing the ground rules of our possible partnership." He moved toward Sherri as he spoke, reaching out to put a gentle hand on her shoulder. "Are you all right?"

Sherri nodded. "I'm fine, really," she said, letting herself be drawn into the shelter of his arm. "But I think I'd like to go home now, Lucas." She looked up at him, as trusting and needy as a small child. "I don't think I was ready for this, after all, and I'd really like to go home."

"Of course," Lucas agreed, speaking in the hushed and gentle voice one uses with an invalid. "I'll take you home right now. Let's just get your purse." He scooped it up off the desk and handed it to her. "Anything else? All right, let's go." He steered her toward the door, leaning around her with one hand to push it open, ushering her through it with the other.

Natalie watched him with her mouth all but hanging open, wondering if this was the same man she'd just been trading glares with. He'd turned from a lion into a lamb. No. No, not a lamb, she amended, a shepherd with his little ewe lamb; suddenly all protective and solicitous, bestowing soft looks and soothing words.

Good Lord, she thought, amazed, *is Sherri the kind of woman he really likes?* Sweet empty-headed Sherri with her big eyes and big breasts and helpless little-girl ways? She would have thought a man like him would be attracted to someone more . . . substantial, but obviously, she'd given him a great deal more credit than he deserved. Men were so disappointingly conventional.

Just then he turned, halfway out the door himself, and caught her eyeing him with vast disapproval and a sort of amused disgust in her expressive brown eyes. "You stay right here until I get back," he ordered. "I'm not finished with you."

That sounded more like the Lucas she knew.

LUCAS RETURNED to Galaxies tired and irritated after having spent nearly two hours trying to soothe his brother's distraught widow. He wasn't the least bit surprised to see that Natalie's car was no longer parked in front of the building. He knew he'd been insane to expect her to comply with his simple request in the first place. "Modern" women had a knee-jerk aversion to doing anything a man asked them to, no matter how nicely he asked; they were afraid someone might accuse them of kowtowing to "the oppressor."

He stalked toward the front doors of the building under a full head of steam, intending to vent his irritation at both women on Rick's files and computer records. He was brought up short by the muted thump of rock music that washed over him as he opened the door.

"What the hell?"

He followed the sound toward the rear office that was its source and, wincing at the assault to his ears, opened the door. For a moment, he wondered if he'd fallen down the rabbit hole. He'd seen this room yesterday when he was familiarizing himself with the Galaxies offices, but yesterday it had been still and silent, the computer screens blank, the video games merely inanimate machines. It had had the same sterile feeling as a million other offices.

Now it looked like a small video arcade. The miniblinds were closed tightly over the windows, blocking out the morning sun, and the overhead fluorescent lights had been turned off. The room was lit only by the flashing lights on the video-game machines and the red, blue and amber spots that pulsed to the beat of the music. Daniel Bishop, certified genius and electronics buff, stood side by side with three children of varying heights and ages in front of the row of machines. Each of them had a hand on a joystick, which they operated with the skill and concentration of Grand Prix drivers.

"Daniel," Lucas said from the door, raising his voice above the level of the music. When that brought no response, he called a bit louder. "Daniel."

He was answered by a shrill, "All-l-l ri-i-i-ght!" and the sound of alternate worlds being destroyed by lightning from a magic laser wand.

Lucas sighed and reached out, feeling along the wall for a light switch. Only the youngest child, a girl of about six, seemed to notice when the lights came on. She looked around, then tugged on Daniel's sleeve.

"Uncle Daniel," she said, her eyes on the large, unfamiliar man who was moving purposefully toward the impressive array of state-of-the-art audio equipment stacked on a worktable. "Uncle Daniel. *Uncle Daniel!*" Her high, childish voice echoed in the sudden silence as Lucas found and depressed the power button.

Alerted at last, Daniel whirled around. His expression as he stared, dumbfounded, as Lucas made him seem barely older than the three kids who manned the other machines. "Oh, Mr.—ah, Sinclair. What are you doing here?"

"I was about to ask you the same thing."

"We're testing."

"Testing?"

"My newest video game. I always bring the kids in to help me test. See how it performs under fire, so to speak. If they don't like it, then it needs more work."

"Good idea," Lucas replied pleasantly. *But does it have to take so many decibels?* "Who's your testing crew?"

"These are my sister Andrea's kids," Daniel explained. "This is Kyle." He nodded at the oldest, then at the other boy, who looked to be about ten. "And Christopher. And this—" he put a hand on the little girl's shoulder "—is Emily. Kids, this is Mr. Sinclair, my, ah, new business partner." He looked at Lucas as if for confirmation.

Lucas nodded. "And it's Lucas," he prompted.

"Of course. This is Lucas Sinclair," Daniel said with more confidence. "My new business partner."

"That was fast," observed Kyle, with the casual callousness and smart-alecky intonation typical of most thirteen-year-olds. "Your old partner is barely cold and you're already movin' in new blood. Way to go, Uncle Dan."

Lucas eyed the gangly young teenager with a look that had caused entire Marine patrols to wish they'd kept their mouths shut. "Your Uncle Dan's old partner was my half brother."

The boy gulped. "Sorry," he mumbled.

"What's a half brother?" asked Emily.

"A half brother is someone you're only, ah . . ." Her uncle looked at Lucas.

"A half brother is someone who has the same mother or father as you do, but not both," Lucas explained in the same gentle tone he had used with Sherri.

Emily responded to that voice in much the same way Sherri had. She moved across the room to look up at Lucas with large, trusting eyes. "Are there half sisters, too?" she demanded imperiously, with a look that said there had better be.

"Sure. Half sisters, too," he assured her, wondering if her Aunt Natalie had deliberately indoctrinated her into the feminist sisterhood or if struggling for equality came naturally to the Bishop women.

"And the half sisters only have a mommy or a daddy, too?" Emily asked, reaching for Lucas's hand.

"No, they have both, just not the same ones. It's like..." He looked down at her, wondering how in hell he'd gotten himself into a discussion on the biology of extended families with a first-grader. "Do you have any friends at school whose parents are divorced?" he asked.

"My mommy and daddy are divorced," she said. "And Daddy married another lady. It makes my mommy cry sometimes."

At a loss for words, Lucas touched the child's hair with a light, almost wistful gesture, brushing it back from her baby-soft cheek. If his ex-wife had agreed to have children, he might have had a little girl just about this age by now. And her life would have been saddened by divorce, he reminded himself, just as Emily's had been. It was undoubtedly for the best that Madeline had turned out to be a selfish, status-hungry Yuppie who preferred making a deal to making a home. But that was neither here nor there.

He dropped his hand, breaking contact with the little girl. "Well," he said briskly, "if your daddy and his new wife have a baby, that baby will be your half brother or sister. Understand?" Without giving her a chance to answer him, he shifted his gaze to Daniel. "I'll be in Rick's, uh, my office for most of the day," he announced. "I'd appreciate it if you'd try to keep the music down to a low roar."

"Yes, of course," Daniel replied, looking about as old as his teenage nephew. "We'll use the headphones."

In Rick's old office—now his, at least temporarily—Lucas found evidence of Natalie. A Post-it note was affixed to the video-display terminal on the desk.

I doubt you'll find anything very interesting in here, but I've just thought of something that could give us the lead we're looking for. I'll tell you what it is when I find it—if you ask me real nice.

Uppity wench! Lucas thought. But he was grinning when he sat down at the terminal and began accessing the files that might offer a clue about his brother's murder. It took him less than a minute to figure out that Rick's password was his wife's name—like most people he'd used something obvious and easy to remember—but four hours later he was no closer to an answer to his question.

He had, however, uncovered some information that cast Rick in a very bad light. Judging by the figures spread out before him, Lucas had very little doubt— none, in fact—that Rick had been embezzling company funds. He'd been at it less than a year, skimming relatively small amounts at first, then larger amounts until, in the week before his death, he'd "redirected" a seven-thousand-dollar chunk of the profits in one fell swoop. He hadn't been very clever or even very sneaky about what he was doing. The trail was so exceedingly simple it was a wonder he hadn't been caught at it long before now. All a person would have had to do was look. But no one had.

As far as Lucas could tell, no one besides Rick *ever* had anything to do with Galaxies's financial records. The invoices all carried his initials to okay payment, the requisitions all came out of his office, the checks all bore his signature. According to the records, Daniel was empowered to sign checks, too, but apparently he never had.

There'd been no need for Rick to be cagey about what he was doing because there'd been no danger of getting caught.

And then he'd gotten killed.

Lucas shook his head in frustration. It just didn't add up. Rick embezzling his own company funds wouldn't compel someone to murder him. It wasn't any kind of motive for murder, which left suicide. But how probable was it that he'd killed himself because he'd been stealing from himself?

Himself and Daniel Bishop, Lucas reflected.

But Daniel didn't know what was going on.

Or did he?

Was it possible that Daniel had known what was going on and had quietly taken care of the problem? But then why would he be so completely unconcerned—unaware, even—that Lucas was digging through his partner's files? If Daniel knew about the embezzlement, then he'd also have to know how easily it would be uncovered. If he knew and had committed murder because of it, he should have been as jumpy as a Marine on night patrol at the mere thought of Lucas prowling through Rick's computer records. Surely he would have made some effort to destroy those records before anyone got near them. But he hadn't.

It didn't make any sense!

Neither did the fact that Rick hadn't used the twenty thousand dollars he'd borrowed from Lucas to balance the books. There was no record at all of that money. Rick had simply gone right on skimming the profits.

None of it makes any sense! Lucas thought, then muttered, "But it will. Before I'm through, it will."

He exchanged disks, inserting another one into the machine, and ordered up the document files. It was more of the same—except for one file that refused to accept Rick's standard password.

Lucas tried it again, carefully typing in the letters of Sherri's name so there'd be no mistake.

Not A Valid Password.

Lucas sat up a little straighter in his chair and typed in Rick and Sherri's wedding date.

Not A Valid Password.

He tried Sherri's birthday.

Not A Valid Password.

"Well, I'll be damned," Lucas said softly, smiling with renewed enthusiasm for the hunt. "A secret file."

7

NATALIE'S IDEA FOR "something that could give us the lead we're looking for" was so simple, she could have kicked herself for not thinking of it sooner. Checking a murder victim's personal financial records for a lead wasn't exactly basic investigative procedure—not like checking for fingerprints at the scene of the crime—but it could be useful when there was nothing else to go on. It did, however, require written authorization from the deceased's next of kin or the weight of a police investigation behind it to convince bank officials and credit-bureau officers to release the records. There were, of course, rather more unorthodox ways of getting the information, but they took more time and effort than Natalie was willing to expend at the moment, especially when help might be only a phone call away.

She dialed her father.

"We're way ahead of you, little girl," he said when she reached him. "Mrs. Peyton gave the authorization when Coffey and Larson were out there the other day."

"Has anyone had a chance to check into it yet?"

"I don't know. Hey! Coffey! You checked into Peyton's bank records yet?" There was a disgruntled snort. "What d'ya mean, Peyton who? How many Peyton cases are you working on?"

Natalie heard a low, unintelligible rumble as Coffey replied.

"Wise guy," her father said, presumably to Coffey, and then, "No, nobody's had time to check it yet."

"What would you say if I said I'd be happy to check it out for you? It'll free up valuable police time for something more important. And I promise a full report."

"You sure you're not working for anybody on this one?" her father asked, knowing full well her first loyalty would be to her client if she were. Not that she would withhold information from the police if she found anything—that would be illegal. She just might not inform them as quickly as she should.

"No, Dad. No client on this one. I told you that already," she said with exaggerated patience.

"Just checking. Hey, Coffey," he bellowed in her ear. "You got any objections to a civilian doin' some of your legwork at the bank?"

Natalie heard a laugh and a short garbled sentence that ended on the upward note of a question.

"Of course, it's Natalie. You ever known me to trust any other civilian with police business?" Coffey's reply made him snort with laughter. "Coffey said to tell you he wants everything you come up with. And that means *everything*, little girl. You hear me?"

"I hear you. Tell Coffey thanks."

The rest of Natalie's afternoon was unproductive in terms of providing her with solid clues to Rick's murder. She found out an awful lot about Rick, though.

He had a tidy little trust fund from his father's estate, although it was much smaller than Natalie would have guessed, given his life-style. His salary from Galaxies was nearly twice what Daniel's was. And he was still living far beyond his means.

His many credit cards were charged to their limits. Two credit lines from separate banks totaled more than he'd make in a year. And, for the past four months, he'd been late on nearly every payment he owed; mortgage on the Lake Minnetonka condo and two car loans included.

If Natalie had been investigating a possible arson—say, the burning of the Peytons' condo, or the Galaxies offices, which she knew were heavily insured because of all the computer and video equipment—she'd have said she'd found the motive. Or even if Rick's death had been proved to be suicide, but—

Or *was* it really suicide, after all? Could Rick have rigged his own death to look like a murder, hoping the insurance would pay off his debts and leave his widow in the clear?

Natalie shook her head, dismissing that thought entirely. The Rick Peyton she knew hadn't been anywhere near that selfless. He'd simply have filed for bankruptcy and started over. There had to be something else. Something more.

Natalie pushed her glasses up on her nose and bent to her task with dogged determination, listing names and amounts, putting check marks next to items she wanted to investigate further, immersing herself in the boring, time-consuming, nitpicky details that made up the bulk of a private investigator's day, until a bank clerk tapped her on the shoulder and told her it was time to go home.

"I TOLD YOU, there wasn't anything there."

Lucas glanced up from the work spread out on the desk in front of him to see Natalie standing in the doorway of his office. She looked as fresh and sassy and sexy as she had that morning when she'd stood toe to toe with him over whatever it was they'd been at odds about.

He, on the other hand, after having spent the entire day hunched over a computer screen without a damn thing to show for it, felt like a limp dishrag. "Oh, there's something here all right. I just haven't figured out how to get to it." His jaw hardened as he turned back to the terminal. "Yet."

Trying not to let her admiration for his tenacity—not to mention his stubbled jaw—show, Natalie advanced into the room and set her straw tote and a paper sack on a corner of the desk. She watched him for a moment, her hands still on her possessions, visually caressing the width of his shoulders and the crisp, dark hair that barely touched his nape and the hair-dusted forearms revealed by the rolled-back sleeves of his shirt.

Why was it, she wondered irritably, that the same long day that had left her feeling washed-out and frumpy, had only served to make him more appealingly male? And why was it that the cobra coiled around his right wrist appeared sexier each time she saw it? And what was it about *her* that made her so susceptible to all of that?

If anybody had asked her three days ago to describe her ideal man, she wouldn't have mentioned any of those things. She'd have said she was looking for someone who combined a healthy scoop of Alan Alda-like sensitivity with a dash of Cary Grant savoir faire, a soupçon of Julia Child's cooking skills and just a pinch—but only a pinch!—of the steely-eyed machismo of Clint Eastwood's Dirty Harry.

So what was she doing drooling over a man who could probably outmacho Dirty Harry, but didn't display a hint of her other three requirements? Well, maybe a hint, she amended; according to what Daniel had said when she'd called about arrangements for dinner, Lucas had shown at least a modicum of sensitivity in dealing with Emily, as well as Sherri.

"Can you cook?"

"What?" Lucas looked up from the keyboard, pretending his annoyance stemmed from being distracted by her inane question rather than admitting—even to himself—that the simple fact of her presence was distracting. "Can I what?"

"Cook."

"Where the hell did that come from?"

Natalie shrugged. "Just curious." She paused. "Can you?"

"I don't starve."

Which meant, essentially, that he couldn't cook. Anyone who knew how to use a microwave and a can opener could keep from starving.

So . . . He'd scored a whopping two on her scale of ideal manhood. Or did a modicum of sensitivity and a ton of machismo even each other out? And what did it matter, anyway? Natalie told herself to quit thinking like a *Cosmo* girl and get her mind back on business.

"What is it you're looking for so diligently?" she asked.

"The damned password to Rick's secret files."

"Secret files? Really?" She came around the desk and perched on the edge, leaning over his shoulder to look at the computer screen. "How can you tell they're secret?"

"Because there's a file on the disk I can't access."

"How do you know there's a special password for it?"

"Because it keeps asking me for one." He turned his head to look at her. The way she was leaning over him brought them practically nose to nose. Lip to luscious lip. "Don't you know anything about computers?" The words were almost caressing in their warmth.

"Just enough to get by," she admitted softly, staring into the depths of his pale green eyes, trying to see something besides her own reflection. She swallowed hard and drew back, folding her arms across her chest in an unconscious effort to put some distance between them. "Daniel set me up with one for my accounts, but even he finally had to admit failure when it came to turning us into real friends."

Lucas sighed, ruthlessly suppressing the urge to reach out and bring her back within kissing distance. "One doesn't make friends with a computer, Natalie. One uses it like the mach— Is that French fries I smell?"

"Might be. Are you hungry?"

"Ravenous," he answered, realizing as he said it that it was true. And not only for her. He'd been glued to the computer all day with nothing but coffee to keep him going, and it was well past the dinner hour.

"I thought you might be." Natalie twisted around to get at the paper sack she'd set on the desk. "Daniel said he didn't think you'd been out of the office all day."

"Daniel? Is he still here?"

"He was when I called to see if he wanted me to bring him something to eat."

"I thought he left when your sister, ah . . . ?"

"Andrea," she supplied.

"When Andrea came and picked up the kids. I haven't heard a peep from his office since then."

"He's always quiet when he's creating. It's only when he's testing that things get noisy." She tilted her head, a small, secret smile curving her lips as she looked at him from over the tops of her glasses. "He said Emily was quite smitten with you."

"Yeah?" The thought was inordinately pleasing. Almost as pleasing as the thought of hearing Natalie say *she* was smitten with him. "I was pretty smitten myself," he said, realizing it was true. "She's a charmer."

"Takes after her Aunt Natalie."

"In more than one way," Lucas agreed dryly, doing his best to hide a grin.

"Oh? How so?"

"She's what? Six years old?"

Natalie nodded.

"And already a radical feminist."

It was Natalie's turn to be pleased. "I do my best."

"Or worst, depending on your point of view. Look—" He held up his hand to stop whatever feminist tirade she was about to deliver. "Are you going to give me some of those fries or just torture me with the smell?"

"Well . . . That depends."

"On what?"

"On just how nicely you ask me." She was already up and moving to the other side of the desk by the time the words were out of her mouth, making his grab for her unsuccessful. "Just let me make sure Daniel gets fed and I'll come back and share the rest with you." She paused in the doorway with one final instruction. "While I'm gone you can make yourself useful and get us both a cup of coffee. I take mine black."

Lucas got up and poured two coffees, as ordered. Carrying them back to the desk, he cleared a space for the two of them to eat, then sat down and waited for his dinner, his mind on the intriguing puzzle of the woman who'd been thoughtful enough to provide it for him even after his sharp words of the morning. He couldn't figure her out at all.

On the plus side, she was gorgeous, feminine and sexy, with great legs and a smile that could melt ice in the middle of a Minnesota winter. She was thoughtful and quick to laugh and obviously didn't carry a grudge. She also made him hard as a frozen pike nearly every time he looked at her. Even when they were squaring off for a bout of verbal warfare, he found himself wondering how it would be to have all that feminine aggression and fire under him . . . again. And completely, this time.

Then he reminded himself of all the minuses that came with her. She was bossy, opinionated, nosy, and far and away too ready to wade into the fray without thinking of the possible consequences. Worst of all was her dedication to her career. After the debacle of his marriage, he'd sworn he'd never, ever get involved with another woman who put her career ahead of everything. *Oh, hell, why just not admit it,* he thought, *ahead of him!*

Not that he believed women shouldn't be perfectly free to have careers, if that's what they wanted. He wasn't that much of a sexist. But why did they have to want one to the exclusion of all else? To the detriment of relationships and families? To—

"Jeez, Lucas, there's no need to look so grim. Here's your hamburger right here." Natalie pulled a paper-wrapped burger out of the sack and put it on the desk in front of him. "And fries." She shook them out onto a paper napkin for easy eating. "And, look," she said, as if she were trying to cajole a grumpy toddler, "little apple pies for dessert. Isn't that nice?"

"Nice," Lucas agreed, smiling in spite of himself.

"I'm glad you approve." She hoisted herself onto the edge of the desk, crossed her legs and unwrapped her burger.

Lucas unwrapped his own burger, wondering idly if her habitual seat of choice was a deliberate ploy to counteract her lack of height. And if she was aware that the position provided a perfect display of her legs, already showcased by those ridiculous high-heeled hooker shoes she wore. He indulged himself for a moment, imagining her in those shoes and nothing else, sitting exactly where she was sitting.

"Stop frowning at my shoes," she said around a mouthful of burger. "And tell me why you haven't cracked Rick's files yet."

He stopped frowning at her shoes to frown at her. "I told you. I still haven't found the password."

"Tell me what you've tried so far. Maybe I can think of something you haven't."

"It isn't quite that easy."

"Try me."

Oh, I'd like to, he reflected. "First, you try the obvious," he said.

"Such as?"

"Nine times out of ten, people will use something that's easy to remember. Their own birthday, an anniversary, a spouse or child's name. Maybe a hobby or the name of the college they went to or their social security number. A little knowledge of the person is usually all it takes to figure out their password."

"I bet you couldn't figure out mine."

Lucas looked at her over the last few bites of his hamburger. "You don't think so?"

"Nope."

"Would you care to place a wager on that?"

"Such as?"

"Oh, say…winner gets one full day of service—with no backtalk and no grumbling—from the loser."

Natalie hesitated. He was, after all, a computer-security specialist; knowing how to crack computer codes was his job. And what did he mean by "service," anyway?

"Chicken?" Lucas suggested.

"Winner gets *reasonable* service," she hedged.

"Who defines reasonable?"

"Webster. And it has to be after we've solved this case on a day to be mutually agreed upon. 'Day' being defined as the time between sunrise and sunset. And you have to guess my code in under ten minutes."

Lucas grinned, already triumphant, and lobbed his balled-up hamburger wrapper into the trash. "I'll do it in less than five," he boasted. Linking his hands behind his head, he leaned back in the chair in a pose of calculated ease and gave her a long, considering look. "You think of yourself as clever," he said, unable to resist the dig. "So it wouldn't be really obvious, like your birthday or your street number or your name spelled backward, but I'd try those anyway, just to cover all the bases. It also probably wouldn't be your social security number. But maybe . . . your license-plate number?"

Natalie shook her head.

"Well, then, let's see. How about your niece's name? Or one of your nephew's? Or the first letter of each?"

Natalie shook her head no after each guess, her confidence in winning the bet growing with each wrong guess.

"Parents' or siblings' name?"

"Nope."

"Then it'd have something to do with your profession. Your private investigator's license number? No, huh? Okay, how about something like P.I. or— What are the slang terms. Dick? No, you wouldn't use that. How about Sherlock? Holmes? Watson? Sleuth? Clue? Gumshoe? Shamus? Ah, I saw that flinch," he crowed, straightening. "Come on, fess up, little girl. Which one is it?"

"Gumshoe," she admitted, her soft mouth twisting up in a wry grimace at how quickly he'd succeeded. Not to mention the annoying fact that he was right; she *had* thought she was being clever when she selected her password.

"Shall we get out the Webster's?"

She frowned at that. "If it's so easy, why haven't you figured out Rick's?"

"Because I've tried all the obvious ones—backward and forward—and none of them worked. I've tried things related to Minnesota—lake, loon, snow, *lutefisk*. Nothing. I tried names of the video games Galaxies has developed. I tried a little pop psychology. You know—mother, hate, Oedipus. I even tried my own name and initials, thinking it might have something to do with the money I loaned him. Still nothing. So I wrote a little program to try anagrams of all the letters in Rick's and Sherri's names." He gestured toward the computer screen. "It hasn't come up with the right one yet. And I don't think it will, because I'm beginning to think the password's something he picked totally at random, like a name out of the phone book or a word in the dictionary."

Something clicked in Natalie's mind. Something that had been subtly nagging at her since earlier that afternoon. She sat up very straight, her hamburger held motionless halfway to her mouth. "Try Dobbs."

"What?"

"Dobbs." She dropped the remainder of her hamburger into the trash. "*D-o-b-b-s.* Today at the bank— That's where I was most of the day, at the bank, going over Rick and Sherri's financial records with a fine-tooth comb. I found two checks made out to 'Cash' and endorsed on the back by someone named Dobbs. They were just for small amounts, a couple of hundred each, but there weren't any notations as to what they were for."

Lucas began typing in the series of commands that would stop the anagram program.

"It's probably nothing." But she knew in her gut that pieces of "unimportant" information were beginning to come together. Maybe. "Rick's neighbor said he was talking to someone on the phone last December, arguing about a football game. He thought the name was Bob or Rob, but it must have been Dobbs. I know it was."

"Will you look at that."

Natalie leaned over Lucas's shoulder to look. The computer had accepted *Dobbs* as the password and was waiting for further commands.

Lucas hit another series of keys, instructing it to print out the entire file, then spun around in the desk chair, propelling it over to the printer. He watched it silently for a long moment.

"Well, I'll be damned!"

Natalie jumped to her feet to lean over him. "What?" she exclaimed, trying to make sense of neat columns of numbers that marched across the green-barred paper. "What is it?"

"Those are dates. And these—" Lucas tapped them with his index finger "—these are dollar amounts." He whistled softly. "Significant dollar amounts."

Natalie grabbed his shoulder with both hands. "What is it?" But she knew. Instinctively, suddenly, she knew.

"It looks like my little brother was up to his neck in gambling debts."

8

"YEAH, I KNOW the name Dobbs," said Nathan Bishop when they brought the information to him. "Marty Dobbs. He's a bookie. He likes to think of himself as a real fancy gentleman." Nathan's tone was mocking. "But he does most of his business out of the back booth at the Lamplighter, downtown. Runs a tidy little loan-shark business on the side to help out clients who may be a little short some weeks. That way he gets 'em coming and going." He frowned and shook his head. "I never would have figured an upstanding Yuppie type like Rick Peyton was mixed up with him. Not in a million years."

"Well, he was," Lucas replied grimly. "Right up to his eyebrows."

"Tipped off by two measly canceled checks," mused Nathan, tapping them against the palm of his hand. He looked up at his daughter and smiled with something halfway between pride and surprise in his expression. "You do good work, little girl. Damned good work."

Natalie beamed, pleased by her father's all-too-rare recognition of her professionalism. "Are you going to arrest him now?"

"For what?"

"For what? For Rick's murder, of course."

"On this?" Nathan snorted and tossed the checks onto his desk. "It isn't even enough to bring him in for questioning."

"But—"

"But nothing. Two canceled checks don't prove diddly-squat, and you know it. Or you should. Hell, they aren't even made out to Dobbs. And you couldn't say for sure it's the same Dobbs if they were. There's gotta be a dozen listings under that name in any phone book in the state."

"But what about the computer printout?" Lucas reminded. "It lists dates and amounts, the odds. Dammit, even the teams he bet on are there! What more do you need?"

"To do what?" Nathan asked calmly. "If you're trying to prove your brother was gambling, you've pretty much proved it. If you're trying to prove Marty Dobbs was his bookie, you maybe—and that's a real slim maybe—could prove it *if* you had some other evidence to back you up. But murder? Not a snowball's chance in hell. You've got no motive, no witnesses, no evidence at the scene—nothing."

"But we know Marty Dobbs had to have something to do with it," Natalie insisted. "Maybe he didn't murder Rick, but he had to be involved somehow."

"Knowing and proving are two different things," her father said. "I know a lot of things I couldn't prove in a court of law."

"Does that mean the police are just going to sit on their hands and do nothing?" Lucas demanded. "Just let this Dobbs character get away with murder?"

"First of all, we don't know that he's been involved in a murder," Nathan stated firmly. "Marty Dobbs may be scum, but he isn't stupid. And killing Rick would be sheer stupidity from his point of view. With the pigeon dead, who's going to pay his tab?" Nathan shook his head. "Dobbs's usual routine would be to send a little muscle out to rough him up a bit if he was behind with his payments, scare him into more regular installments. But I've never heard of Dobbs being involved in murder."

"There's a first time for every—" Natalie began.

Lucas silenced her with a hand on her arm. "And second of all?" he prompted, in that soft voice that raised the hairs on the back of Natalie's neck.

"And second of all," Nathan continued, meeting the hard look in Lucas's pale green eyes with one of his own, "the police aren't going to just sit on their hands. I'm going to give this information to Coffey and Larson and they're going to follow up on it."

"And?"

"And the rest is police business," he finished. "We'll keep you posted on our progress."

"But, Dad—"

"But nothing. Now get outta here, both of you, and let me get back to work."

"I'LL JUST HAVE TO GO down to the Lamplighter myself," Natalie said ten minutes later. They were sitting in Lucas's Jeep, waiting for a light to turn green.

"Go down to the what?"

"The Lamplighter. That place Dad mentioned, where Dobbs does his business. I assume it's a restaurant or a bar of some sort. I'll just go down there and ask around a bit."

"And say what?" Lucas inquired sarcastically, unleashing his frustration on her. He raised his voice to a falsetto. "Please, Mr. Dobbs, sir, did you have Rick Peyton murdered?"

"Give me a little credit, will you? I won't even mention Dobbs or Rick or any of—" she waved her hands "—this whole mess. I'll just go in, have a drink, mention to the bartender that I'd heard a person could get a little action in his place." She shrugged. "Then see what happens."

"He'll probably think you're a hooker."

"I don't look the least bit like a hooker."

He glanced down at the open-toed high-heeled pumps she wore. "In those shoes you do."

Natalie looked down at her feet. Her shoes were lovely; a deep peach with the throat and toe openings rimmed in ivory. They were an exact match for her peach chemise dress and loose ivory blazer. "Just what have you got against my shoes, anyway?" she grumbled, turning her foot this way and that to admire it. "It took me days to find just the right color to match this dress."

"They make you look like some damned ice-cream sundae or something, just waiting to be gobbled up."

"Yeah?" Natalie looked up, pleased. He'd just paid her a compliment, whether he knew it or not. She wondered briefly if she should apprise him of that fact.

"Pull over," she said instead, motioning toward the curb.

"What for?"

"There's a phone booth. I want to check the Yellow Pages for the Lamplighter's address."

Lucas drove right past the phone booth and on down the street, straight toward the highway entrance ramp.

Natalie gave him an angry glare. "Do you have a better idea?" she challenged.

"Yes, as a matter of fact, I do. *I'll* go down to the Lamplighter."

"And do what? Call everyone to attention and demand they tell you what you want to know? Or just bash a few heads together until something falls loose?"

"At least I can protect myself if anything happens."

"Well, nothing *would* happen if I went down there."

"And how do you figure that?"

"Because people don't get hostile and make things 'happen' unless they're threatened in some way. And I'm the least threatening person I know."

"Says who?" Lucas muttered.

Natalie ignored him. "I've never had any problem with violence, and I've been in some of the very worst parts of town investigating fraud and arson cases for insurance companies, or tracking missing persons." She shifted on the seat, angling her body to face him more fully. "I once traced a missing teenage girl to a suspected crack house and just walked right in and brought her out with no problems at all."

"You were damned lucky," Lucas remarked, shuddering at the thought of Natalie in any sort of danger at all. She might have the ambition and drive of a man, but she was still a woman. *All* woman. And a small one, at that.

"No, I'm damned good at my job," she declared fiercely. "Besides, if worse ever came to worst, I have this." She reached into a specially constructed pocket in her purse and pulled out a .38-caliber revolver.

Lucas very nearly ran off the highway. "For Chrissake, Natalie, put that away. Guns are nothing to play with."

"I don't play with it," she said tartly. "I have never played with it. My father taught me better than that. When he finally realized I was going to be a private investigator, no matter what he thought of the idea, he decided I'd better know how to defend myself. Before he gave me this gun, he made sure I knew how to use it." Her smile was small and deliciously self-satisfied as she slid the gun back into its special compartment. "He still doesn't know whether to be bust-his-buttons proud or royally p.o.ed about the fact that I'm a better shot than he is," she added, giving the bulge in her purse a fond little pat.

Lucas's only answer was a disbelieving grunt that, unfortunately, put Natalie in mind of her father.

"If you'd care to indulge in a little contest of skills, I'd be glad to oblige," she suggested, feeling her dander rise at yet another macho male's assumption that because she was small and female, she was helpless. "There's a public rifle range not too far from here."

Lucas refused to rise to the bait.

"Bet I can outshoot you."

Stone-faced, Lucas kept his eyes on the road.

"Chicken?" she prodded.

"All right, you asked for it. Where's the range?"

"SAME TERMS as last time," Natalie announced as they approached the firing line. "Winner gets one full day of cheerful, uncomplaining, reasonable service from the loser."

"How'd 'cheerful' get in there?" Lucas growled. "I don't remember that from last time."

"Okay, strike 'cheerful,' if it'll make you happy. It won't matter, anyway."

"Why not?"

"Because when I win—"

"*If* you win."

Natalie rolled her eyes. "If I win, the bets will cancel each other out and no one will owe anyone anything."

"And if I win?"

"Then you'll get two days of slave labor." She shot him a challenging grin. "But it isn't going to happen, so don't get your hopes up." She held her revolver, barrel down, in her right hand and flipped open the cylinder with her thumb, twirling it to check the ammunition. "One round apiece," she said, snapping it closed. "In case of a tie—" her expression showed him how likely she thought that was "—we'll take one more shot each. And just to show you how fair I am—" she extended the gun to him, butt first "—I'll let you take a couple of practice shots to get the feel of my gun."

"That won't be necessary," he said, declining her offer, as she'd somehow known he would. "You go ahead." In a parody of good manners he extended his hand like a maître d'. "Ladies first."

Knowing he expected her to object, Natalie gave him her sweetest smile and stepped up to the firing line. Taking a minute to adjust the protective headset to a comfortable position over her ears without skewing her glasses, she raised the revolver, her right hand around the grip, her left forming a cradle for gun butt and wrist. "Are we considering the head or the heart the bulls-eye?" she asked.

"The head, by all means. It's a smaller target."

Natalie nodded in agreement and, after taking careful aim, squeezed off the first shot. A small hole appeared on the paper target, right between what would have been the eyes if the target had had them. She allowed herself a small, satisfied smile and then fired five more shots—carefully, precisely, slowly; placing them all within inches of the first one.

Lucas stood behind her, watching. But he wasn't watching the target. His eyes were on Natalie—on her blond hair, blowing softly against her neck in the summer breeze, on the way her slender shoulders tensed in anticipation of the recoil, on the wide-legged stance she'd taken to achieve the best balance possible in the gravelly soil. It pulled the skirt of her narrow silk chemise dress tight, outlining the curve of her buttocks and the long slender line of her thighs, drawing the eye downward to the swell of her nylon-clad calves and her elegant little feet in those impossibly sexy, fantasy-inspiring high-heeled shoes.

I don't care what she calls them, he thought. *They make me think of sex. Down-and-dirty, sweaty, satisfying sex. With her.* And if that wasn't the definition of *hooker shoes,* he didn't know what was.

"Your turn." Natalie slipped the padded ear protectors from her head and turned from the target, a wide smile of triumph on her face. "Lucas? It's your—"

He swooped down on her without warning, like a cobra striking out at its prey. Taking her into his arms, he lifted her off her feet and pressed her close. One hand cupped the back of her head, bringing her mouth up to his. His tongue plunged between her parted lips, taking, tasting, ravaging, as hot and heady as the best imported brandy.

Natalie hung there like a rag doll, her arms at her sides, the empty gun in one hand, the protective headset in the other, too stunned to react.

And then it was over.

Just like that.

He let her slide to her feet, running his hand down her arm to take the gun as he stepped away. Without a word, without looking at her, he reloaded, lifted his right arm parallel to the ground and fired six rapid shots at the target.

Natalie winced as each bullet exploded from the gun; she stood there with the protective headset dangling uselessly from her fingers and her eyes wide with surprise and arousal. She watched him stride down the length of the firing range and tear the paper targets from their posts to compare them, then turn and come striding back toward her with the tense, measured steps of a gunslinger coming down the middle of some dusty street to answer a challenge. She could almost hear the jingle of spurs.

He was aroused, too, she realized, as she stood there watching him stride toward her—blatantly, powerfully aroused. The navy blue fabric of his conservative summer-weight suit did little to hide his condition; he did nothing at all to either hide or flaunt it.

Natalie felt herself soften, deep inside, as her body prepared itself—without her consent or approval—to accept him. If he took her in his arms again . . . if he kissed her. . . if he even so much as touched her. . . she'd end up flat on her back on the firing range, begging him to take what she was dying to give.

He handed the targets to her instead. "You win," he said, ignoring the clamoring of his body, urging him to finish what he'd started. "By a hair."

Natalie swallowed and held on to her composure, also by a hair. "You're better than I expected," she remarked coolly, adjusting her glasses to look down at the bullet holes in the targets as if they made perfect sense. She couldn't have said, just then, which one was hers.

"So are you," he returned equally coolly, wondering why in hell he was putting himself through this torture. He shouldn't have kissed her again, shouldn't have reminded himself of how much he liked the taste and feel of her. But he'd watched her shoot, self-confidence and daring in every sleek line of her. She was as tempting as sin on a hot Saturday night, and he'd suddenly understood the meaning of an "irresistible impulse" — way down at the visceral level.

He wanted her. Still. Now. Immediately. Always and all ways.

She, on the other hand, stood there, cool as the first daffodil of spring poking its head up through the melting snow, calmly studying bullet holes in a couple of damned paper targets!

"I'd almost be inclined to call it a tie," she said, still looking at the targets. "If you hadn't admitted defeat first." She rolled up the targets and stuck them under her arm as if she didn't have a concern in the world beyond the results of their little contest. "May I have my gun, please?" she asked tightly, her eyes still downcast to hide the desire she knew he would see if she dared to look at him.

He handed it to her without a word, waiting patiently, his frustration well hidden, as she wiped it off, reloaded it, double-checked the safety and carefully put it back into her purse.

"Ready to go?" he asked, as if nothing had happened. If she wasn't going to mention the kiss, then, by damn, neither was he.

Natalie nodded and led the way to his Jeep, hoping she wouldn't stumble in the loose gravel and ruin her Oscar-caliber performance.

DANIEL LOOKED UP from the phone when they walked through the front door of Galaxies. "I'm glad you're back," he said, completely unaware of the complex, unexpressed emotions shimmering between the two of them. He thrust the receiver at Lucas. "It's Sherri," he told him. "This is the third time she's called. I can't get any work done," he complained to his sister as Lucas took the receiver from him. "I wasn't going to answer it this time, but she let it ring and ring. It was breaking my concentration. Jana usually puts it on the answering machine when she leaves, but—"

"Did he say who he was?" Lucas asked tensely, speaking into the receiver.

Natalie waved her brother to silence.

"No, that's all right. Sherri, listen to me. Calm down and call the police," Lucas instructed. "Ask for one of the officers handling your case. Coffey or—" He looked at Natalie for the name.

"Larson."

"Coffey or Larson," he said to Sherri. "Tell him exactly what happened, every word you remember." He paused, listening. "No, don't wait for me to get there. Do it now," he ordered. "Don't cry. Sherri, no...don't cry. Look, the sooner you let me hang up, the sooner I'll be there. Yes, I promise. Yes."

Natalie could see the impatience simmering in him, hear it clearly in his voice, and wondered why Sherri couldn't hear it, too.

"*Yes*, Sherri," he replied through clenched teeth. "Now, hang up and call the police. I'm on my way."

"What happened?" Natalie demanded.

"She got some kind of threatening call about some money Rick owed."

"Dobbs?"

"She doesn't know." He was already moving toward the front door as he spoke. "But who else would it be?"

He paused, his hand on the metal handle across the middle of the glass door. "You coming?"

Natalie shook her head. "It sounds like you can handle this one on your own." And no way did she want to have to stand around and watch him hover over dear, sweet, helpless Sherri. "Besides, I've got to head over to my office and take care of a few things."

9

NATALIE PULLED UP across the street from the Lamplighter and sat studying it for a moment before getting out of the car. It was just as seedy and disreputable looking as she'd expected it to be, given its location and the activities that allegedly went on inside.

She flipped open the file folder on the seat beside her to take one more look at the information she'd dug up over at Records. Marty Dobbs's mug shots showed an average-looking man. He had a narrow face, a sharp chin and rather large, round eyes, thereby disproving, Natalie reflected, that old saw about beady eyes and a criminal mentality. He also had a small mole on his left cheek, a dapper little mustache and a forty-dollar haircut designed to camouflage a receding hairline.

His rap sheet wasn't especially long, considering. He'd been picked up for questioning in connection with illegal gambling activities half a dozen times, but had been released without being charged. He'd gone to trial—once—when one of his runners turned state's evidence in exchange for a deal but that hadn't stuck, either. He apparently did some pimping on the side. But there was nothing to indicate that he was in any way prone to violence. She knew he was capable of it, of course; most criminals—most *people*—were, if someone pushed them to it.

Her plan was to do nothing that could possibly be construed as pushing.

Checking to make sure her gun was right where it should be, Natalie took a deep breath, slung her purse strap over her shoulder and slid out of the car. Walking across the street toward the Lamplighter, she could feel the adrenaline building with each tap of her heels against the pavement.

The heavy door swung open easily, admitting her into the dark, smoky atmosphere of the bar. She stood just inside the entrance, letting her eyes adjust to the difference between twilight and gloom, her gaze flickering innocently over the patrons for a few moments after she could clearly see them. There were less than a dozen men sitting at the small round tables in the center of the room and at the bar. The backs of the booths—four or five of them along the longest wall—were too high for her to see if they were occupied. A basketball game was in progress on the TV behind the bar, the colorful images flickering in the dim light, but only one or two men seemed to be watching it. The bartender was leaning on an elbow, talking quietly with a customer, both of them seemingly unaware of her presence. Everyone else was looking at her. Natalie took another deep breath, told herself she was perfectly safe and started toward the bar.

Someone must have signaled the bartender, alerting him to her approach, because he looked up, did a slight double take at the sight of her and began moving down the bar. "You lost?" he asked when he was close enough, making it more than obvious that women like Natalie were seldom seen in the Lamplighter.

"No, not lost." She stepped up onto the barstool with as much grace as possible, letting the straps of her purse slide off her shoulder to the crook of her elbow as she laid it on the bar. She gave the bartender a level look. "Just thirsty."

The bartender shrugged, as if, having made one effort to warn her off, he was now absolving himself of any responsibility. "What'll it be?"

"Jack Daniel, straight up, no ice." She ordered her father's drink without missing a beat, having decided ahead of time that her usual white-wine spritzer wouldn't go with the image she was trying to project.

"That'll be three-fifty," the bartender announced as he set the drink on a tiny white napkin in front of her.

She laid a ten-dollar bill on the bar. "I've heard a lady can get a little action here," she said softly.

"Could be. Depends on what kinda action you're lookin' for."

She put another ten-spot on top of the first. "The kind of action Marty Dobbs is in charge of."

The bartender gave her another look. "You sure you wanna see Marty?"

"Positive."

"Okay." He slipped the two tens off the bar and into his pocket. "Hey, Cal," he hollered. "The little lady here says she wants to see Marty."

"Yeah?" The man named Cal eased himself out of one of the booths and stood. He was big and beefy, with the wedge-shaped body and overly-developed shoulders and chest of a dedicated bodybuilder. His pale blond hair was very short, brushed up in one of those trendy cuts that made the wearer look as if he'd stuck his finger in a light socket. His muscle T-shirt was black, one size too small. His jeans were so tight, Natalie found herself wondering how the blood got to his legs. He had a tiny skull dangling from his left ear.

He swaggered over to where Natalie sat, the smarmy smile on his face telling her he was obviously one of those men who were under the mistaken impression that women everywhere found them irresistible. She smiled, trying to make him think that she was one of them as he slid onto the barstool next to her.

He leaned in, too close. "What business you got with Marty, sweet thing?" he asked, reaching out to stroke a finger down the back of her hand where it lay on the bar.

Natalie forced herself not to jerk away; to play the game exactly the way she'd mentally rehearsed it. "A friend of mine told me that Mr. Dobbs—" *That was a good touch,* she thought. *The Mr. Dobbs.* "Ah . . . that he takes bets."

"Bets?"

"Yes. On, umm, football and . . . things," Natalie murmured, finding she didn't have to do much to feign the nervousness she'd decided would be appropriate for a woman in her supposed situation. Cal and his stroking finger were enough to make anyone nervous. She reached for her drink, unobtrusively ridding herself of his touch, and took a sip. It burned all the way down. "Is Mr. Dobbs here?"

"Maybe he is and maybe he isn't."

Natalie shifted on her barstool, both to put some distance between herself and Cal, and to take a quick look into the booth he'd vacated, in the hopes of sighting her reason for subjecting herself to the less-than-savory atmosphere of the Lamplighter. "I'd really like to see him if he's available."

Cal shifted, too, maintaining the distance and blocking her vision. "See him about what?"

Natalie widened her eyes, giving him her best innocent look. "Are you his secretary?"

"Yeah. His secretary." Cal snorted, amused. "I'm his secretary and nobody gets to see him without I know what they want."

"Well, my friend said he might—"

"Who's this 'friend'?" Cal interrupted.

"Just a friend," Natalie said quickly. "She asked me not to use her name. Her husband wouldn't like it if he knew she was gambling with the household money again." She smiled placatingly, lifting one shoulder in a little shrug. "You know how husbands are."

Cal's smarmy smile widened. "Yeah, I know how husbands are." He leaned in a little closer—so close she could feel his beery breath on her cheek. "You got a husband, sweet thing?" he asked, running his finger down her arm.

She felt her skin contract with revulsion under the sleeve of her ivory jacket. "Well, I . . ." Deliberately, Natalie let her uneasiness show, hoping to convince him she was exactly who she said she was by giving him what he seemed to expect. He struck her as the kind of man who would enjoy knowing he made people uneasy, especially women. "Yes," she admitted finally, with seeming reluctance. "Yes, I have a husband."

"He the jealous type?" His finger moved up and down her arm.

"Yes. Very." She shuddered, again having to do little acting to call up the appropriate reaction. "He'd kill me if he knew I'd been in here."

Cal curled his fingers around her biceps, deliberately brushing the backs of them against the side of her breast. "We'll just have to make this our little secret, then, won't we?"

"Secret?" Natalie questioned, looking up at him with wide eyes as she stalled for time, busily sorting through her options. It was obvious that Cal wasn't going to do any talking about his boss until he thought he'd established some sort of sexual deal with her in exchange for the information.

She could go along with him for a while longer, hoping things wouldn't go too far before she found out something useful about Marty Dobbs. Or she could pretend she'd changed her mind about gambling and leave right now, before she'd really learned anything, possibly saving herself from an unpleasant scene when he realized she wasn't going to come across.

Leaving was probably the wisest choice, but it was really no contest. She wouldn't find out anything if she turned tail and ran. Odds were she could count on the presence of the other patrons in the bar to keep him from actually assaulting her. If worse came to worst, she reasoned, she had her gun.

She decided to play his game a little bit longer.

She took a sip of her drink. "What secrets are you talking about—" she touched her tongue to her upper lip and let her lashes flutter upward, as if she were sneaking a shy peek at him "—Cal?"

"Oh, I think you know, sweet thing," he replied, his eyes glittering with sexual excitement. "It's a real big secret. You're gonna like it a lot." Still holding her arm, he straightened a finger and rubbed the back of it over her nipple. "Why don't we go outside to my car and I'll show it to you. It's parked right out back behind the bar."

"Really, Cal," she said, forcing herself to smile coyly as she shifted away from his touch. "We hardly know each other."

His hand tightened on her arm. "We could remedy that real easy, sweet thing."

"Sure. Sure, we could," she agreed, trying to edge away from him. She moved her hand, oh-so-casually, to the clasp of her purse and flicked it open. "But wouldn't you like to buy me another drink, so we could talk awhile? I like to talk to a man . . . first."

"We could talk in my car." He slid off his barstool, pulling Natalie off hers, and wrapped a beefy arm around her waist.

She barely had time to react before he'd pulled her to him. "Cal, please." She put her hands on his shoulders and pushed. "Let's not rush things."

Cal obviously wasn't in a mood to take his time. He pulled her closer.

Fighting the instinctive urge to stiffen and pull away, Natalie forced herself to soften against him. As she expected, he took advantage of her lack of resistance to push her back against the bar, pressing his body more fully into hers and bending his head.

She turned her head away from his kiss, intent on maneuvering the open purse dangling from her elbow into a position where she could grasp it. She felt the wooden edge of the bar bite into the middle of her spine. Dimly, just as she managed to snag her purse, she heard a lone catcall and a sharp whistle and the bartender's voice from the other end of the bar. "If you and the lady wanna get amorous, Cal, take it outside. I don't allow screwing in here."

It was then that the first prickle of real fear slithered down Natalie's spine. Cal was so damned big! And so intent on his purpose. And incredibly, it looked as if no one in the bar would object if he actually tried to drag her outside.

Blindly, firmly telling herself to be calm—to keep calm—she groped, one-handedly, for the special compartment in her purse, her head still turned so his wet, foul kisses landed in the curve of her neck. Her mind was reeling with visions of all that could happen if she didn't extricate herself from the situation . . . fast.

"Come on, sweet thing," Cal whispered against her neck, sliding a hand up to cover her breast. "Don't pretend you don't want it."

She grasped the gun butt at last, just when she thought she'd never find it, and curled her forefinger around the trigger. Almost fainting with relief, she brought her hand up and jammed the gun, still inside her purse, hard against his rib cage.

His ardor died a quick and satisfying death. "What the—" he began, his arms loosening their hold on her.

He whirled away, his hands leaving her abruptly. There was another oath—not his—and a loud crash, then he was sprawling at her feet. Incredulous, she looked down at him, then up, ready to thank her rescuer and assure whoever it was that rescue hadn't been necessary.

"What in *hell* do you think you're doing in here?" Lucas bellowed, grabbing her by the upper arm. "Have you lost whatever good sense you may have had?" he demanded, before she could open her mouth to answer his first question. He shook her once, hard, then began dragging her toward the door. "Have you gone completely, stark-raving crazy?"

"Hey, man, that's our buddy you just laid out on the floor there," someone said, stepping in front of them.

Lucas came to a halt, stopping so abruptly that Natalie stumbled against him. He righted her with a quick, upward jerk, his attention focused completely on the speaker. "Get out of my way."

"Lucas," Natalie said in warning, her gaze focused on the two men coming up behind them.

Lucas ignored her. "You heard me, fella," he challenged the man blocking his way.

"Lucas," Natalie repeated.

"If you know what's good for you, little girl, you'll keep your mouth shut," he told her without looking at her.

"Lu—" The rest of the word was lost as one of the men yanked on her other arm in an effort to tear her from Lucas's grasp.

At the same moment, the man blocking the door lunged forward, obviously intent on inflicting severe bodily harm. Lucas lifted his arm in a quick, twisting motion, letting the man's weight and forward momentum do most of the damage as his chin connected with Lucas's upthrust elbow. He was already reeling backward from the blow, crashing into an empty table, as Lucas turned, quick and deadly as the cobra on his wrist, and drove his knuckles into the breastbone of the man who'd dared to put his hand on Natalie. The man fell to his knees, clutching at his chest as he gasped for air.

"Anyone else?" Lucas snarled. The pure come-on-I-dare-you cussedness in his glittering green eyes told them all he'd relish the opportunity to hit someone else.

The other patrons eyed him for a long moment. Apparently what they saw convinced them they wanted no part of the man who'd laid out three of their drinking buddies without breaking into a sweat.

"Hell, no!" Someone finally broke the tense silence. "Take her the hell outta here. She looks like she's more trouble than she's worth, anyway."

"You got that right!" Lucas barked and hustled her toward the door at a fast march.

Natalie stumbled along beside him, practically on tiptoes, as he propelled her over the sidewalk and across the street, her open purse dangling from her elbow as she tried to straighten her glasses.

"You can let go now," she gasped, as they came up alongside his Jeep. It was parked right behind her gray Ford. "Lucas." She tried to pry his fingers loose. "Lucas, let go. You're cutting off the circulation to my fingers."

Jaw clenched, he jerked open the passenger door and tried to toss her in.

Natalie balked. "Lucas, let go of me!" she ordered.

"Get in."

"Lucas—"

"Just get in, Natalie. I'm taking you home."

"I've got my own car."

"Leave it."

"In this neighborhood?"

"Natalie . . . I'm warning you. Get in or I'll—"

"Or you'll what? Get in or you'll what?" She yanked her arm out of his hand and took a step back. "Knock me stone-cold like you did those guys in there?"

A small muscle in Lucas's jaw bulged. "Don't tempt me," he warned through clenched teeth.

"Oh, that's right. Threaten me with violence."

"Natalie, dammit, get in the car before those goons change their minds and decide they want you, after all."

Natalie refused to budge. "I am sick and tired of being treated like some helpless little girl who can't take care of herself," she said in exasperation. "First my father, and now you. Well, I won't stand for it! Do you hear me?"

"The whole block hears you."

"I will not stand for it! I can take care of myself just fine. I *was* taking care of myself until you barged in like the Marines at Iwo Jima and started bashing heads to—"

"It sure as hell didn't look like you were taking care of yourself to me! It looked to me like that guy was—"

"I'm a trained private investigator," she bit out, ignoring him as if he hadn't spoken. "I have a license on the wall of my office that says so. I carry a gun and I'm trained to use it. A fact," she reminded him, "that you should be well aware of."

"So why didn't you?"

"I don't need some man with a Rambo complex thinking he needs to—"

"Why didn't you use your gun?"

"I *was* using it. I had it pressed against his ribs." She stepped into him suddenly. "Like this," she said, and jammed her purse into Lucas's midsection with the full force of her anger.

"For Chrissake, Natalie," he growled, going very still as he felt the barrel of the gun against his ribs.

"That was pretty much his reaction, too," she remarked with satisfaction, savoring the feeling for a moment before stepping back. "Now, I'm getting into my car," she said calmly. There was no trace of her anger, except in her eyes. "And I'm driving to my house . . . without any help from you." Not waiting for his reply, she turned on her heel and headed for her car, dismissing him.

He watched silently as she walked the half-dozen steps to her car and unlocked the door. "Drive straight to your place," he told her as she opened it to get in. "I'll be right behind you."

Natalie slammed the door shut and gunned the engine to life, peeling away from the curb as if she'd just seen the starting signal of the Indy 500.

She was almost home, with Lucas right behind her in his black Cherokee, when the reaction to the past half hour really set in. Part of it was fear; the instinctive, feminine fear of knowing what could have happened to her back there in that sleazy bar. She had the gun, yes, and she knew how to use it—was fully prepared to use it—but even streetwise cops sometimes had their guns taken away from them. Even cops sometimes ended up hurt. Or worse. She could handle fear, though. She'd *been* handling it just fine, dammit! Until Lucas came charging in to rescue her.

It was perfectly justified, frustrated anger that made her hands shake on the wheel and hot tears slide down her cheeks. She blinked rapidly, trying to clear her vision. Women like Sherri Peyton cried, dammit! Not women like her. She never cried. *Never.* But the tears were still sliding down her face as she turned into her driveway.

Slamming the car into Park, she jumped out as if the devil himself were her passenger, and went running for the front door, determined not to let Lucas see what she knew he would interpret as a sign of inherent feminine weakness—or, worse, a ploy to gain his sympathy. But he was too fast for her.

"Natalie?" His hand closed over her shoulder as she was struggling to fit her key into the lock. "Dammit, Natalie, we have to talk about this."

"I don't want to talk about it," she retorted, trying to shake him off. "Go away."

He refused to be shaken. "Natalie, look at me." He yanked her around by the shoulder. "I have a few th—" His insides tightened like a vise. "Good Lord, what's wrong?" He cupped his hand under her chin and turned her face up. "Are you hurt?" His jaw tightened. "Did that bastard hurt you?"

"You're the only bastard who hurt me," she snapped, then jerked her chin out of his hand and turned away from him again. Twisting the key in the lock, she got the front door open. "So just go away and leave me alone!"

He followed her into the house. "*I* hurt you? How?" He put both hands on her shoulders and turned her to face him, searching for any sign of damage or injury. "Where?"

Natalie glared up at him through her tears, too angry to guard her words. "My pride, okay? You hurt my pride! Charging in there like I was some witless, helpless child who couldn't be trusted to take care of herself. I've been fighting that kind of attitude all my life, starting with my father. And I just can't take it from—" she sniffed "—from you. I won't."

"Natalie." He cupped her cheek in one hand, with the beginnings of a tenderly indulgent, understandingly amused masculine smile on his lips as he prepared to soothe her ruffled feathers. "I never meant to hurt your feelings, baby. I was just try—"

She slapped his hand away. "You didn't hurt my feelings, dammit! I'm not crying because you hurt my feelings. I'm crying—" she wiped at her eyes, dashing away the wetness "—*was* crying because you made me mad as hell!" she told him, seething with frustration. "And you're still making me mad." She turned her back on him, moving out of the hallway and into the kitchen. "So why don't you do us both a favor and get out of my sight before I forget I'm a nonviolent person!" She threw her purse on the table as she spoke, turning her head toward the door to glare at him.

Their gazes touched, and locked, and they stood for a long, tense moment, unmoving, as something invaded the charged air between them, subtly changing and adding to the atmosphere of anger and frustration.

"Go on!" Natalie burst out, trying to deny the jolt of sexual excitement that pierced her like a lightning bolt as he stood there looking at her with that intent, fascinated expression in his green eyes. "Get out of here."

But he'd seen the leap of excitement in her eyes, too, instantly recognizing it for what it was because it so perfectly mirrored the feeling suddenly zinging through his body. Passion. Mind-boggling, blood-boiling, hot and fiery passion. She stood there—flushed, furious, excitingly provocative—issuing the silent but unmistakable challenge of a woman deliberately daring a man to take what she offered.

Lucas had never been one to back down from a challenge.

He moved toward her with his swaggering gunslinger's walk—slowly, his eyes never leaving hers, stopping only when he was close enough to reach out and cup her shoulders.

Natalie lifted her chin, haughty as an Amazon queen. "I told you to leave," she said, refusing to take a single step back. Instead, she put her hand in the middle of his chest and pushed. "I meant it."

"No, you didn't." Still holding her gaze with his, he took her hand and dragged it slowly—giving her every chance to pull away—down his flat stomach to his groin. "*Did* you?"

Her fingers curled around his erection and squeezed gently. "No," she agreed softly, still glaring at him. "I didn't."

They stared at each other for another long, charged second. Two pairs of eyes filled with heat and fire. Two sets of lungs heaving with emotion. Two hearts beating a rapid tattoo of need. Two people full of hot, roiling, damnably confusing feelings with only one logical place for them to go.

10

THEY MOVED AS ONE person, coming together hungrily. His arms wrapped around her waist like steel bands as he bent his head to hers. Her hands went around him, under his suit coat, holding on as tightly as she could. Their lips touched, burning hot and parched for each other. Their mouths opened, avidly seeking the sweet wetness within. Their tongues touched and retreated and returned to touch again, each of them savoring the unique, longed-for taste of the other.

It was wonderful, but it wasn't enough.

Natalie rose on tiptoe, angling her head to accept more of his kiss, flattening her breasts against his chest. She slid one hand down his back, spreading her palm over his firm buttocks, and pulled him to her, hungry to feel the hard ridge of his erection pressed against her.

It still wasn't enough.

She bent one knee as high as the narrow skirt of her chemise dress would allow, sliding it up along the outside of his thigh. *Better*, she thought muzzily, drugged by his masterful, mind-numbing kisses, but still not nearly enough, even with his hands moving down to cup her buttocks, kneading them as he obligingly lifted her into him. She moaned and murmured his name against his lips.

"I know, baby," he growled softly. "I know. It isn't enough."

He set her on her feet and ran his hands up her back and around to her shoulders, slipping them inside the collar of her blazer. She dropped her arms, wriggling out of it, then raised them behind her, reaching for the zipper of her dress. She felt his breath, hot, heavy and unsteady, against her neck as they both fumbled to remove her dress. A moment later it was off, drifting down her body to pool around her feet on the floor, and he was reaching for the front fastener of her bra.

Frantically, as desperate for the sight and feel of his skin as he was for hers, Natalie reached for the buttons on his shirt, only to stop, shuddering with passion as his hands closed over her bare breasts. They both sighed at the exquisite feel of his hard palms against her giving softness. And then he rolled her nipples between his thumbs and forefingers, and she shuddered again and raised her arms, reaching up to clasp his neck and bring his head to her deliciously aching breasts.

Lucas stopped her with his hands on her wrists, holding her arms outspread so he could look at her.

She was peaches and cream, exuding exquisite, feminine heat, and all but pulsing with her desperate need of him. He let his gaze wander slowly, savoring her smoldering, passion-drugged eyes, her flushed cheeks and her moist coral lips, half parted with the rapid soughing of her warm breath. The luscious swells of her breasts were crested with pebbly, peachy-pink nipples.

Her ivory skin glowed with vibrant health, and her strong, slender torso curved temptingly with every move she made.

Gently, he drew both arms behind her, grasping them in one big hand at the small of her back, and arched her over his arm. He ran his other hand down her body, slowly, his fingers spread wide, from the little hollow at the base of her throat and over her breasts, so that his thumb and little finger brushed across her nipples.

Natalie shivered and cried out, but then held very still, mesmerized by the glitter of desire in his pale green eyes and the erotic dance of the cobra on the back of his hand as it drifted, feather light, down her body.

His fingers traced the lacy edge of her French-cut ivory-pale panty hose, then drifted down over the slight curve of her belly to the half-hidden triangle of hair at the apex of her thighs. Turning his hand, palm up, he slipped it between her legs and cupped her. He could feel her through the lacy fabric, hotter than he'd ever imagined a woman could be. It nearly knocked him to his knees.

Natalie's knees *did* buckle. She sagged against him, as her mouth blindly sought his flesh, her wrists twisting in his grasp in an effort to free herself so she could touch him. "Lucas." She bent her knee again, lifting it high to wrap her leg around the back of his, opening herself more fully to his touch. "Oh, Lucas, please."

He slipped his hand under the waistband of her panty hose, sliding it down her stomach again and back between her legs. She was incredibly soft and wet against his palm, her body quivering with need and excitement, her hips moving as she sought a deeper, more satisfying touch. Trembling with his own need, his own towering excitement, Lucas answered her wordless plea with a rough thrust of his tongue between her lips and a gentler—but not *too* gentle—thrust of his fingers between her legs.

Natalie peaked immediately, nearly shrieking, her whole body clenching as she arched upward. She lifted her other leg, nearly climbing him in her effort to get closer, and he let her hands go, slipping his under her buttocks to hold her, pressing her tight against him as the spasms of her climax rippled through her.

"Again," Lucas murmured into her neck when she stopped shivering. "I want you to do that again." He bit lightly at her shoulder, almost sending her into another tailspin. "But I want to be deep inside you when you do. I want to feel you coming with more than just my fingers."

"Yes," Natalie breathed softly. "Oh, yes, I want you inside me, too." She uncrossed her ankles and slid her legs down to the floor. "I want you naked and inside me."

She took his hand and led him—both of them were still trembling and eager—down the dark hall to her bedroom. "Don't move," she said, letting go of his hand as they came to a stop beside the bed. Turning from him, she quickly switched on a small, pink-shaded lamp and turned back the bedcovers to reveal flower-strewn sheets. She took off her glasses and shrugged out of the straps of her bra. Kicking off her high-heeled shoes, she hooked her thumbs into the waistband of her panty hose, skimmed them down her legs and stepped out of them.

Then, gloriously naked, she turned to face him again. "Your turn," she said with soft fierceness, reaching for his shirt buttons. "I want you as naked as I am."

She undid the buttons with feverish haste, tugging the shirt from his pants, pushing the fabric off his broad shoulders to bare his chest to her gaze and the quick, damp touch of her lips on his warm, hair-dusted skin. Fascinated, eager to see more, to taste every part of him, she abandoned his shirt, leaving him to finish twisting out of it, as she turned her attention to his belt buckle.

There was the soft whisper of leather sliding against leather; the rasp of a zipper; a husky moan and a rumble of strained male laughter. "Natalie." He caught her busy little hands in both of his. "Baby, you're going to leave me standing here in my shoes and socks with my pants down around my ankles and my body pointing at yours." He tried to smile, but it came out more like a grimace as she eluded his grasp and gently caressed him through his briefs. "Quite a comical sight, so I'm told," he finished raggedly. "And I don't think my ego could stand hearing you laugh just now. Let me finish undress—"

Natalie knelt abruptly, sliding her hands down the back of his legs as she did so. "Lift your foot," she said, placing her hand under his heel.

Lucas acquiesced quietly, awed and a little humbled by the sight of Natalie kneeling at his feet. His ex-wife would have slit her wrists with her gold card before putting herself in such a position. And yet, Natalie, even more of a "modern" woman, apparently saw nothing damaging to her dignity in getting down on her knees to rid him of his shoes and socks.

She reached up, grasping the waistbands of his trousers and briefs, and pulled them down to his ankles. "Not such a comical sight," she said softly, looking up at him with warmth and admiration in her wide brown eyes. "It's actually quite . . . impressive from this angle," she added, stroking his masculine ego with her words as she stroked the underside of his straining erection with the tip of her finger. Then she chuckled. "Not that I can see much without my glasses." She reached behind her, pretending to grope for her glasses on the bedside stand.

Lucas laughed, too, and hooked his hands under her arms to pull her to her feet and into his embrace. Toppling them both over onto the bed, he kicked his feet free of his pants and underwear. They rolled over the covers like two rambunctious children, laughing and breathless over nothing in particular, until, suddenly, they were staring into each other's eyes, not laughing anymore, but still breathless.

"You're an incredible woman, Natalie Bishop," Lucas murmured softly, and covered her mouth with his.

It was a kiss of hunger they shared—wet and ravenous, accompanied by moans and sighs, nibbling bites, catlike licks and greedy, suckling motions. It traveled from lips to cheeks, down arched necks, to broad, hard shoulders and fragile collarbones, from the delicate peak of a full, soft breast, to the hard little masculine nipple buried in a mat of crinkly brown chest hair. It explored the hills and valleys of two yearning bodies; warm lips nibbling at the smooth, satin skin of a quivering tummy; small white teeth nipping at a hairy thigh. Fingers were kissed, and toes, elbows and ears and everything in between until they met again—lip to lip, heart to madly beating heart, man to woman.

She sighed and, pulling him to her with her hands on his shoulders, parted her legs in welcome.

He groaned and, cupping her buttocks in his palms, thrust himself home.

The mating began—easy and measured at first, as they let passions smolder. Their hips rotated almost languidly and their breathing was deep and slow as they shared kisses that were drugging and impossibly, incredibly sweet. And then someone picked up the pace— he or she, or both of them together—taking it faster and further, until they were thrusting wildly, madly, clutching at sweat-slick skin, panting for each labored breath, striving together toward the ultimate pleasure.

Natalie peaked first, by a second or two only, her keening cry and arching body signaling to Lucas that he could let go, too. And he did, groaning as if mortally wounded, his muscled torso twisting up and away from hers as his back bowed under the overwhelming onslaught of pure, primitive satisfaction. For a moment, he felt as if he should throw his head back and howl in triumph, proclaiming his possession to anyone within hearing distance. Only the nagging thought of how the woman beneath him might react to such a blatant display of masculine prerogative stopped him.

He lowered himself against her instead, carefully taking the weight of his heavy torso on his forearms to prevent crushing her. He hadn't thought about it a moment ago—he hadn't been thinking about *anything* then except the driving need to satisfy his passion, and hers—but now he wondered if he mightn't have squashed the breath out of her. She hadn't uttered a sound since the shriek when she climaxed, and she lay beneath him now, unmoving, with her eyes closed and her hands lax upon his shoulders.

He brushed the backs of his fingers gently over her cheek. "Natalie? Are you all right?"

A wide smile curved her lips. "Oh, I'm *wonderful*," she said dreamily, without opening her eyes. "Ab-so-lute-ly wonderful."

Lucas chuckled. "That you are, little girl. That you most definitely are."

AN HOUR LATER they were sitting in Natalie's kitchen, eating the dinner that neither of them had made time for earlier.

"You really *can* cook," Natalie said admiringly, staring down at the two halves of the perfectly browned grilled-cheese sandwich he'd just set in front of her. It was accompanied by a rather limp dill pickle and a handful of almost-stale potato chips—all he could find in her sparsely stocked cupboards.

"You haven't tasted it yet."

"I can tell just by looking. My sister, Andrea, says half the secret of cooking is making it look good. This looks great." She took a bite, careful of the gooey cheese in case it was still too hot. "Tastes great, too. You can come here and cook for me anytime." She looked up over the tops of her glasses, giving him a roguish grin as he set his own plate on the table. "Too bad there isn't some tried-and-true method of keeping men in the kitchen."

"Method?" He slid into the seat across from her.

"You know, the old saying?" She nodded her head toward his feet. "Barefoot and—"

"Pregnant," he finished for her in a strangled voice.

Natalie paused with her sandwich halfway to her mouth, startled by his very odd expression. "What's the matter?"

"I didn't use anything. Birth control," he explained at her blank look. "I didn't use anything for birth control." How could he have been so stupid and uncaring! "I didn't even think of it."

"Oh, is that all?" She took a healthy bite of her sandwich. "Don't worry about it."

"Don't worry about it? Natalie, babies happen from what we just did."

"And, hopefully, will do again," she added teasingly, giving him a lascivious look. She wiggled her eyebrows. "Soon."

"It's nothing to joke about," he said sternly.

"No, you're right, it isn't. I'm sorry. But it's nothing to worry about, either. You may not have used anything—" she popped a potato chip into her mouth "—but I did."

"You did?"

"Well, of course." She gave him a mildly exasperated look. "You don't think I'm going to leave something as important as birth control to someone else, do you?"

"Well, no, but—"

Her look of exasperation deepened into borderline disapproval. "You're not one of those men who thinks a woman who's prepared is some sort of loose-limbed floozy, are you?" The expression in her eyes said he'd better not be.

"Certainly not," he replied, insulted that she would think so.

"Well, then, what's your problem?"

"It's just that it's been my, ah, experience that most women expect the man to take care of things."

"I'm not most women," Natalie snapped, disliking the thought of his doing with other women what he'd just done with her, and wondering just how many others there'd been in his hell-raising past.

"No, you're not most women." It was a fact he found himself continually adjusting to. "But, still, don't you think you should have told me?"

"Told you what? That I wear an IUD? Besides—" she gave him a narrow-eyed stare "—you didn't ask."

"I should have."

"Yes, you damn well *should* have."

They glared accusingly at each other across the table for a moment and then Lucas sighed. "Are we fighting?" he asked in a playfully plaintive voice.

Natalie's lips twitched. "I think so. Almost."

"About what?"

She grinned at him. "Beats me."

"Then let's stop it." He reached across the table and squeezed her hand. "Okay?"

"Okay," she agreed, returning the squeeze.

They ate in ponderous silence for a few minutes, with nothing but the sound of chewing and swallowing between them.

"Does this mean we don't have anything to say to each other if we're not arguing?" Lucas questioned.

"Why don't you try telling me what's hidden under that blacked out paragraph in your military file," she suggested. "We probably won't argue about that."

Lucas grinned at her over his sandwich. "We will when I tell you it's classified."

"Couldn't you just give me a hint?"

"I already did. Cryptographics."

"Yeah, right," she scoffed. "All that kung-fu fighting you did in the bar came from lessons in cryptographics."

"You're bound and determined to cast me as some super-secret spy with an opposite number in the KGB, aren't you?" Lucas shook his head. "Well, it wasn't anything like that. No double oh seven. No kill or be killed. Just some very tedious, frequently boring code work that the government prefers to keep secret."

"And the kung-fu stuff?" she asked suspiciously.

"Basic Marine training."

"So you say," Natalie mumbled, refusing to give up her thrilling fantasy of danger and derring-do quite so easily.

Lucas shook his head in amused exasperation and applied himself to the last two bites of his sandwich.

Natalie stared at him for a thoughtful moment or two, wondering if that's all there really was to his government service. She shrugged, resigning herself to the fact that she might never really know for sure. "So," she said, picking up her own sandwich again, "what happened at Sherri's?"

"What happened at Sherri's when?"

"This afternoon after we got back from the shooting range. She was all upset because Dobbs called her. Remember?"

"It wasn't Dobbs. At least, I don't think it was."

"Who was it, then?"

Lucas shrugged. "From what she said, it sounded like your average collection call. 'Hello, Mrs. Peyton, your overdue account has been turned over to our agency for collection and we'd like to know when we can expect payment.' That kind of call."

"Did they actually say it was about an overdue account?"

"I don't know." He crunched a stale chip between his teeth. "Sherri was too upset to remember exactly."

"I'll bet Coffey had plenty to say about that. He'd hate going all that way for nothing."

"He didn't say much, actually. He and his partner got there shortly after I did. When it was finally clear the only thing Sherri really knew for sure was that someone was claiming she owed them money, and that there was no new evidence to implicate Dobbs, or anyone else for that matter, in anything, they thanked her politely for calling and hightailed it out of there so fast you'd think somebody was trying to offer them a bribe."

"Coffey has a thing about hysterical women. Dad says he'd rather face a spaced-out addict with an M-16. I take it Sherri *was* hysterical?" she asked, more cattily than she intended.

"Not hysterical, but pretty darned upset," Lucas replied, giving her a look of mild reproof. "And can you blame her? Not only has she lost her husband, she's been left with a mountain of debt. From what she said, I gathered that call was the first she'd heard about any of it."

"That doesn't surprise me," Natalie said. "The bank account is in Rick's name. He made out a monthly check to Sherri for 'Groceries and Incidentals,' according to the notations." Her tone made it very clear what she thought of the arrangement. "I assume she just used a credit card for anything else she bought, or she asked her loving husband and he gave her the money for what she needed."

"I take it you don't approve?"

"Do you? Honestly?"

"Honestly? Well…" He'd honestly never really given it much thought before, but he was inclined to think it certainly had to be better—with a few adjustments, of course—than the cold-blooded arrangement he and his ex-wife had had. At Madeline's insistence, they'd had separate accounts, separate funds, separate everything, with each of them paying a percentage of basic living expenses according to their separate incomes, as if the marriage were an arrangement between room-mates.

"*Please* don't tell me you approve," Natalie continued when he sat there thinking about it. "Lord, you *do* approve, don't you?"

"Is it really all that bad?"

"Is it really all that bad! Lucas, think about it for a minute," she said indignantly. "Put yourself in the wife's place. All your money in your husband's name. You have no idea what you have or what you owe. You get an *allowance*, for heaven's sake, as if you were a child. And you have to ask if you want to buy a new dress or a pair of panty hose or a . . . a magazine that isn't covered under 'Incidentals.' How would that make you feel?" She could feel herself working up to a tirade, but she couldn't help it. It was a pet peeve of hers. More than a pet peeve: It made her see red. "Even if you were given whatever you asked for, whenever you asked for it, how would it make you feel to have to ask? And what would happen if your husband died, like Rick? You just said Sherri had no idea what kind of financial difficulty she's in. Is that right? Or fair? She doesn't know what her assets are, what she owes. I'll bet you she doesn't even know how much the mortgage is on that fancy lakeside condo." Natalie shook her head in disgust. "Any woman who lives with that kind of arrangement is just asking for trouble."

"Did something like that happen to you?" Lucas asked quietly. She was a tad too vehement for her anger to be on behalf of oppressed women in general.

"Not to me," Natalie admitted. "To Andrea."

"Your sister?"

"Andrea's a throwback to the fifties. Or was. She was in the top five percent of her class with offers of scholarships to two colleges, but she married her high-school steady two weeks after graduation—with my father's full approval, I might add—and settled into a life dedicated to being a perfect wife. She did her husband's research and typed his papers all through college. She gave wonderful little dinner parties to help him advance his career. She went to the opera instead of movie musicals because that's what he liked. She dressed the way he wanted her to dress, thought the way he wanted her to think, and even spaced her children according to his schedule. She did everything she thought she was supposed to, and she never, ever, overspent the weekly budget he set for her. And then," she continued bitterly, "about three years after Emily was born, he said she was 'smothering' him and ran off to California with some little birdbrain bimbo half his age."

"What happened to Andrea?"

Natalie sighed. "She lost everything. Her husband, her home, her standard of living, her standing in the community, her self-respect."

"I'm sorry."

"She's doing pretty well now, considering. She and the kids moved in with Dad. He'd been rattling around in the house by himself for years, anyway—my mother died shortly after Andrea got married and then Daniel and I moved out—so it's a good deal for everyone. She's working part-time and going to vocational school part-time. She's going to be a plumber."

"Plumber?" Lucas was incredulous. A vision of the woman he'd met when she stopped by Galaxies to pick up her kids flashed through his mind; he couldn't quite make it fit with his idea of what a plumber was supposed to look like.

"The pay and benefits are excellent," Natalie informed him. "Far better than what she'd get working in an office. She'll have it pretty well made when she starts work, especially if she manages to start her own business. But she'd have been far better off if she'd never let herself get into a position of total dependency in the first place."

"Yes, I see your point. All too clearly." Clearly enough, in fact, for him to have gained a smidgen of insight as to what might have helped make his mother the way she was. "And to answer that question you asked a while ago: No, I don't approve of husbands handling all the financial affairs and treating their wives like children. But someone has to handle them, otherwise nothing would ever get paid."

"Agreed."

"So what's the solution? Separate everything, as if a married couple were no more than roommates sharing the same living space?"

"There's such a thing as joint accounts, you know. And two people sitting down, deciding together what they're going to do with *their* money. Most households run on two incomes these days, and even if a man brings home a paycheck while the woman stays home to look after the house and kids, it doesn't mean he's entitled to make all the decisions. It's a partnership. They both contribute. They should both have a say in the decisions. And they should—"

"All right. All right." Lucas held up his hands in mock surrender. "You've convinced me. Completely."

"You're not just saying that to get me to shut up, are you?"

"No. I agree one hundred percent with everything you've said." *And that fact alone amazes the hell out of me.*

"Well, I'm glad. Because it's important to me." *Because I'd hate to think I'd gone to bed with that much of a male-chauvinist oinker!*

"Obviously."

"But I still think—" She broke off, laughing at herself when he grimaced and covered his ears. "All right. I'll get down off my soapbox. No more speeches." She twirled her empty plate around and flashed him a saucy grin, more than willing to forget a subject that depressed her as much as this one did. "At least for the rest of tonight."

"Good. Because I've got plans for the rest of tonight. And if I have my way, they definitely won't involve a lot of talking." He pushed his plate aside and put his elbows on the table. Leaning across it, he waited until she leaned in to meet him before he continued. "Unless you want to talk dirty to me—my plans could be altered to allow for dirty talking." Somehow, with the inflection of his voice or the look in his eyes, he made it sound like a dare.

Natalie rose out of her chair, leaning halfway over the table, and crooked her finger at him, motioning him to lean closer, too. She put her lips next to his ear. "Lucas, my sweet," she began. The frank, unadorned words that followed wiped the teasing grin right off his ruggedly handsome face, replacing it with a glazed look of pure lust. "And that's a promise," she said. "But only if you can catch me." She jumped up and made a mad dash for the kitchen door.

He leaped out of his chair with a roar and caught the back of her robe in his fist. Natalie squealed, yanked at the loose knot in the belt, and kept going, leaving him with a handful of bright blue silk and a glimpse of her naked back as she disappeared down the hall. With a muttered oath, Lucas threw the robe aside and raced after her.

She ran through her bedroom into the adjoining bathroom—where she grabbed a towel off the rack for cover—and on into the connecting second bedroom she used as an office, which connected with the hall again, making a loop that brought her up behind Lucas. She nearly crashed into his back. She squealed a second time—a high-pitched, feminine sound of excitement, executed a quick turn and raced back the way she'd come, slamming doors as she went in an effort to slow him down.

Twice they raced from bedroom to bathroom to office, through the hallway and back again—the slamming of doors accompanied by shouts of breathless laughter and threats of what would happen when he caught her. And then, suddenly, it was deathly quiet.

Natalie stopped in the bathroom for a moment, panting softly, her heart racing, and listened for a noise that would tell her which way he was coming.

There were no footsteps. There was no heavy breathing. Nothing. But she knew he was coming, sneaking up on her. She could feel it. She stood in the middle of the bathroom, her tingling skin about to burst with excitement, knowing he would come crashing through one of the doors any minute. But which door? Her eyes darted back and forth, searching for a sign.

And then she saw a shadow of movement.

Quickly, she ducked behind the door he would come through, holding her breath, waiting for just the right time to make her getaway. The door burst open, nearly smashing her flat, except that she'd dropped her towel and put her hands up, ready for it.

"Aha! I've got . . ." His voice faded as he realized the bathroom was empty. "You."

Natalie forced herself to stand still, waiting . . . waiting. . . . Judging the moment just right, she tiptoed out from behind the door, into the bedroom and then the hall, down past the office door. Grabbing the doorknob, she slammed it closed, hoping to mislead him into thinking that's where she'd gone, then sprinted down the hall and into the darkened living room. Diving soundlessly over the back of the sofa, she rolled to the floor and under the coffee table. Lying there on her stomach, she tried to calm her breathing and her nervous giggles of anticipation.

She knew he'd find her, eventually, but it was going to take him a while to figure out where she'd disappeared to. Sooner than she'd expected, though, she heard him come creeping down the hall.

"Oh, Nat-a-lie...."

She heard him moving around the kitchen and the sound of cupboard doors opening and closing, as if he thought she might be hiding under the sink.

"Nat-a-lie."

He was in the open archway between the dining and living rooms.

"Nat-a-lie, my pet. It will go much easier for you if you just give yourself up."

She held her breath, watching his bare feet as they approached her hiding place. *He can't see me*, she told herself as they moved on by the coffee table. *He can't see—*

"Gotcha!"

She yelped in surprise and delicious fear as his hand closed around her ankle and dragged her out from under the low table.

"It would have been much, much better if you'd come when I called," he said, flipping her over onto her back. "Now you're going to have to pay." He had a knife in his upraised hand.

Natalie sucked in her breath and let loose a scream that could have curdled fresh milk.

Lucas tossed away his weapon and covered her mouth with his hand, cutting her off midscream. "Jeez, Natalie, it was only a butter knife!"

She stared at him in the dim light, her eyes wide above his restraining hand.

"I didn't mean to scare you like that, baby." He took his hand away from her mouth slowly, in case she decided to scream again. "Are you all right?"

Natalie's frightened eyes suddenly danced with pure devilment. "Scared the hell out of you, didn't I?"

"Probably scared a few of your neighbors, too," he said, his eyes laughing back at her. "I wouldn't be surprised if one of them called the police to report a murder in progress."

Natalie sobered instantly. "Do you think so?" She scrambled to sit up. The last thing she wanted was to have to explain to one of her father's cronies how she came to be buck naked in the middle of her living-room floor with a butter-knife-wielding maniac straddling her hips. "Let me up!"

Lucas shook his head. "You made me a certain promise," he reminded, pushing her back down with a hand on her chest. "A number of promises, actually—" he reached out with his other hand and removed her glasses, setting them out of the way on the coffee table "—regarding a very personal service that would be rendered if I caught you. Well—" he cupped a breast in each hand, thrumming the nipples with his thumbs "—I caught you. And I'm not letting you up until you keep your promise."

"I always keep my promises," Natalie murmured, completely forgetting about the neighbors or the police or anything but the man who was leaning over her with passion glittering in his beautiful green eyes. "I'm a great believer in keeping promises."

She reached down and, for the second time that night, unzipped his zipper. He wasn't wearing any socks or shoes or even underpants to make things difficult. And he rolled over onto his back, docile as an over grown puppy, when she pushed, making no protest at all when she came to her knees beside him and began, with the delicate precision of a cat, to caress him with her tongue.

She started with his ears, slowly tracing the whorls, darting inside, then out again to flick at his lobes. She followed the straining tendon of his neck downward, lapping her way over his collarbone to the hollow of his throat, dragging her tongue down the center of his beautifully hairy chest. He was breathing hard by the time she finished teasing his tiny male nipples into hard little points of sensation; moaning by the time she'd finished tasting the quivering flesh of his washboard belly and the intriguing hollow of his navel; groaning when she finally put him out of his misery and took him into her mouth.

He'd never had a woman make love to him so completely, so unselfishly, so enthusiastically, so...*lovingly* before. For all his experience, he'd never really had a woman make love to him at all, he realized. And he didn't know if he was going to be able to stand it much longer.

"Natalie." He reached for her, touching her silky hair with trembling fingers. "Natalie." He couldn't seem to say anything else; couldn't think of another word besides her name. "Natalie."

She lifted her head to look at him, smiled a siren's smile rife with the knowledge of her feminine power, and straightened, throwing her leg over his hips. She sank down, impaling herself on his rigid maleness. Dropping her head back, she savored the feeling for a moment, loving the way he filled her to overflowing; loving, too, the ragged groans and tortured breathing of her lover as he struggled mightily for control. And she took it from him—deliberately—moving slowly, rotating her hips, rising and falling, until her own control fled with his and they were falling over the edge of sanity into an ecstasy of pleasure—together.

11

THEY WERE in the bathroom the next morning, after having made laughing, steamy, slap-and-tickle love in the shower, before Natalie thought to ask him how he'd known she was at the Lamplighter the night before.

"I've figured out how your devious little mind works."

She raised an eyebrow at him in the mirror.

He grinned. "And one of your contacts down at Records is a stoolie," he admitted. But his first reason was true, too. Uncanny as it was, he did seem to know how her mind worked—at least some of the time—which .very nearly scared him to death. "Someone from Records called your father to let him know you'd been checking up on Dobbs."

"That new prison matron they've got down there, I bet," Natalie fumed as she smoothed her hair into its usual sleek style. "She looks like the stoolie type."

"Whatever you say," Lucas said, concentrating on his reflected image, trying not to cut himself to bits with an unfamiliar razor and nothing but soap to soften his beard. "Anyway, your father called me to say he thought I'd like to know what my 'partner' was up to and that, incidentally—" he raised his voice to make himself heard as Natalie disappeared into the connecting bedroom to finish dressing "—if I valued my life, I'd get my butt down there and make sure his little girl had some backup in case things got to be too much for her to handle." Nathan Bishop had also mentioned how glad he was to have someone else watching out for his wayward daughter, but Lucas didn't think it would be wise to mention that.

"Remind me to thank the old busybody for his concern!" Natalie hollered from the bedroom. "*After* I chew his ear for interfering in my life—" she came back into the bathroom, tucking a jade-green blouse into a narrow, matching skirt "—again." She sighed, and began rummaging through her makeup bag for her lipstick.

"Can you really blame him?" Lucas certainly couldn't; if she really was his responsibility, he'd want to keep her wrapped in cotton batting. "Someone's got to worry about you," he said, bending over to rinse the last of the soap from his face so he could get out of her way. "You have a habit of getting yourself into trouble when there's no one—" The last few words were muffled by a towel as he dried his face.

Natalie paused, her lipstick pencil poised over her upper lip. "I beg your pardon?" she said, knowing she wasn't going to like what she heard.

Lucas slung the towel around his shoulders, leaned against the doorjamb and crossed his arms. "You have a habit of getting yourself into trouble," he repeated.

"Yes, I heard that part." She finished outlining her mouth with precise, abrupt movements. "I don't agree with it, but I heard it." She snapped the top back on the pencil and picked up her lipstick brush. "I have a feeling I'm not going to like the rest of it, either, but let's hear it, anyway."

"You have a habit of getting yourself into trouble when there's no one around to—" he knew she wasn't going to like it; but, tough, it was true "—curb your wilder impulses."

"You curb dogs or children," Natalie informed him tartly, wiping off the brush with a tissue and dropping it into her makeup bag. "Not adults. And I am an adult, completely responsible for myself and my impulses, wild or otherwise."

"I didn't mean it that way."

"Yes, you did," she insisted, brushing past him on her way back into the bedroom. "You meant it exactly that way."

Lucas hitched up his towel and followed her. "Don't look now, Natalie," he said, trying to tease his way out of it, "but I think we're arguing again."

"Damn right, we're arguing," she replied, refusing to be teased. "And we will continue to argue every time you try to pull that macho I'm-doing-this-for-your-own-good routine on me." Putting a hand on the closet door for balance, she jammed her feet into a pair of jade-green heels that matched precisely the color of her silk blouse and slim skirt. "If I don't let my father get away with it, I'm sure as hell not going to let you."

"Didn't last night mean anything to you?"

"Yes." She yanked a pale lavender silk jacket off its wooden hanger. "It means I should have been more careful." She thrust her arms into the sleeves. "It means

I should have covered my tracks a little better, so you couldn't follow me into the Lamplighter and louse things up before I had a chance to find out anything." She stepped back from the mirrored door and surveyed her image, pausing to straighten a lapel. "And it means if I'm ever faced with a similar situation I'll certainly handle it differently. But it *doesn't* mean you—"

"That's not what I meant."

"No? What did you mean, then?"

He looked her straight in the eye. "Don't you think last night gave me some rights your father doesn't have?"

Natalie rolled her eyes in disgust. "Isn't that just like a man?" she said to the ceiling. "No, last night does not give you any rights," she said to him. "Not if by 'rights' you mean some sort of control over my life. We slept together and it was very nice—" *the understatement of the century* "—and I'd like to do it again." *And again.* "But, it doesn't change anything," she told him, wondering why it felt like a lie. "I'm still a completely autonomous individual, as are you. As my partner on this case, I may consult with you before I do something connected with it and, then again, I may not. But I will *never* ask for your permission. Is that clear?"

"As a bell," he replied through clenched teeth.

"Good." She grabbed a light tan leather shoulder bag from the bed and opened it. "I have a breakfast appointment with a client," she announced, fishing around inside the purse, "so I can't wait around for you to get dressed." She pulled out her key ring, slipped a single key off and tossed it onto the bed. "Lock the door when you leave, will you?"

She marched through the bathroom and into her office, pausing to pick up a file she'd need for her meeting, and continued on to the front door. Her furious progress came to a halt on the front porch—not because her temper had cooled but because Lucas's Jeep was parked behind her car in the driveway. She tapped her foot impatiently, considering her options, and then stomped over to her car, opened the door and plopped herself down behind the steering wheel. All Lucas had to do was put his clothes on; he'd be out in a few minutes. Waiting and glowering was, in her opinion, a better alternative than slinking back inside to ask him to move his Jeep. Especially after the great exit she'd made.

She crossed her arms and fumed while she waited.

What on earth was the matter with her? Falling into bed with —*Okay, okay,* she placated the nagging conscience that insisted on pointing out that it could hardly be described as falling. So why had she practically *dragged* a man like Lucas Sinclair into her bed?

She knew he was all wrong for her. Had known it from the minute she'd laid eyes on him in Rick Peyton's den. He was another one just like her father—a rough, tough ex-Marine, the original macho man who clearly thought the "little woman's" place was squarely under some man's thumb. Oh, all for her own protection and well-being, of course. She snorted in half-amused disgust as the thought formed. As if any man were actually going to admit he kept a woman on a leash for *his* benefit!

No doubt about it, a relationship with Lucas Sinclair would mean one long, ongoing battle for her independence as a thinking, reasoning, self-sufficient woman.

So, dammit, why did she still find him so irresistibly attractive? And what was it about him that had her thinking of him at odd moments during the day and dreaming about him at night? And why, oh, why, did she continue to want him with an intensity that frightened her?

She pounded a fist on the steering wheel. She was *not* like her sister. She wasn't! And she wasn't like Sherri Peyton, either, or any of the other thousands—even millions—of women in the world who made themselves over or gave themselves up for the love of a man.

She was not in love with Lucas Sinclair.

Was she?

"No," she said aloud, in the mistaken belief that saying it would make it true. "No, I'm not."

Love had nothing to do with whatever had brought them together. They had nothing in common but an uncommonly strong "lech" for each other, the uncanny ability to annoy each other at the drop of a hat, and a case to solve.

And when the case was solved?

Natalie didn't want to think about what would happen when the case was solved, because thinking about it gave her an oddly empty feeling in the region of her heart. She pressed down on her car's horn to keep from thinking about it, emitting a long, loud, impatient blast of noise at the house.

How long did it take a man to put his pants on, anyway?

Lucas appeared on the porch a good five minutes later, looking endearingly rumpled and devastatingly sexy in the clothes that had spent most of the night on her bedroom floor. He tossed her a sour grimace—for her use of the horn, presumably—then turned and made a show of closing and locking her front door, taking what she considered an undue amount of time to accomplish the simple task.

Natalie eyed him warily as he came down the walk toward her car with his gunslinger swagger. She just knew he was daring her to say something about the length of time it had taken him to finish dressing when he knew she couldn't go anywhere until he moved his car. She bit her tongue, giving him the satisfaction of nothing more than a glare when he bowed slightly, mockingly, and presented her house key between his thumb and forefinger.

She snatched it out of his hand, tossing it onto the seat beside her without a word, and turned her head sharply, with a disdainful lift of her chin, dismissing him as she leaned forward to turn the key already sitting in the ignition. Gunning the engine to life, she revved it slightly to emphasize the fact that he was still keeping her waiting.

She watched him return to his Jeep in her sideview mirror. Watched him climb into it and calmly, with no wasted motion or apparent frustration, put it into gear and back out of her driveway.

Five minutes later, when he'd completely disappeared from sight, Natalie was still sitting in her driveway, her hands wrapped around the steering wheel, hated tears trickling forlornly from under the rims of her glasses.

Was this really how the most wonderful, important, satisfying night of her life was going to end?

LUCAS FORCED HIMSELF to drive at a sane and sensible speed, despite the fact that he wanted to stomp the pedal to the floorboard and fly down the road like some teenage Romeo who'd just had a fight with his girl. Because that's exactly how he felt—like a crazy, mixed-up kid whose girlfriend had just told him she didn't want to go steady anymore, then wouldn't tell him why.

And, dammit— he bounced his fist off the steering wheel to emphasize his point —*I don't even like her.*

But he knew he lied. He liked everything about her— except her damned maddening independence—very much. Way too much. So much so that he was beginning to suspect he might even be falling in love with her. That he'd—heaven help him!—already fallen in love with her.

When had it happened?

Sometime last night when she was making him feel like a sultan with an entire harem at his disposal? He'd like to think it had happened then, because, if it had, he could talk himself out of it. Sex wasn't love. It might feel like love sometimes—especially when it was happening or when you were outrageously turned on by the woman. But, eventually, the heat died down and, if you were much over twenty-one, you knew it had only been lust and wishful thinking, after all.

The trouble was, with Natalie it had begun to feel suspiciously like love *before* they shared the most incredible night of sex he'd ever experienced.

He'd gotten his first real clue yesterday afternoon at Sherri's when he'd found himself praying for patience and silently comparing her cloying helplessness to Natalie's spunky never-say-die attitude. It had been quite a shock to his system, realizing the woman he'd considered the archetype of ideal femininity was, in reality, a giant pain in the butt. He'd actually found himself suggesting—diplomatically, of course—that she might want to try taking a few courses in simple bookkeeping to help herself out of the mess in which her husband had left her.

Then Natalie's father had called, alerting him to the fact that his "partner" might be getting herself into more trouble than she could handle down at the Lamplighter. Instead of sensibly suggesting that Nathan take care of it—she was, after all, his daughter—he'd gone charging down there himself, like some idiot knight bent on rescue, and found her backed against the bar by a beefy Neanderthal.

And then, he thought furiously...and *then* she'd had the gall to throw his chivalry back in his face, berating him for trying to keep her from getting hurt! He'd wanted to strangle her for being so stupid, and cradle her in his arms to keep her safe, and kiss her senseless—all at the same time. He'd never felt like that about anyone. Looking back on it, he realized he'd been a goner long before they'd finally made love.

Whatever! However! It had happened.

But, dammit. His fist bounced off the steering wheel again. *I don't have to like it.*

Sexy little Natalie Bishop, with her inbred ability to annoy the hell out of him, and her hooker shoes and her maddening aversion to giving up control of any part of her life to a man, was going to mean nothing but trouble.

So why, he wondered, was he looking forward to the future with such a feeling of satisfaction and eager anticipation?

NATALIE FOUND HERSELF at something of a standstill in her investigation of Rick's murder. She'd gotten just about everything she could from checking the records available to her; she knew his banking habits, his credit history, what insurance policies he'd carried and in what amounts. She'd made use of one of her many contacts and would soon be in possession of a record of his telephone calls, for both the office and his home, for the past six months. But that was going to take a few days, at least, and she felt as if she needed to do something in the meantime.

If not for Lucas's clumsy interference the night before, she might have been able to head back down to the Lamplighter and continue trying to make direct contact with Marty Dobbs, but that was out of the question now. Having departed the scene with a man who busted up tables and left three men flat out on the floor wasn't likely to earn her any kind of welcome there anytime soon.

She was too . . . something . . . to sit still. Unless otherwise occupied—and even then, as she'd realized during her business breakfast—she tended to stare off into space, recalling the pleasures of the previous night with Lucas and wondering how soon they might be repeated.

Thoroughly annoyed with herself, she went back home to her office after her breakfast meeting, determined to type up the last report she'd dictated to herself. It was on an alleged insurance fraud that had turned out to be a perfectly legitimate stolen-property claim.

She typed the report and made a call to the insurance company to let them know it was on the way. She even made a few calls to get the ball rolling on her investigation into every facet of Marty Dobbs's miserable life. And then she gave in to temptation and wandered into her bedroom. She gazed longingly at the bed where so many wonderful things had gone on the night before.

"Damn it all!" she chided herself in disgust. She realized she'd actually picked up the pillow Lucas had slept on to breathe in the scent of him.

Throwing the pillow down as if it were on fire, she hurried back through her office, checking to make sure the answering machine was on, and left the house.

What she needed was action, she decided, getting into her car. Something definite to do that would get this case moving forward and keep her wayward mind off Lucas Sinclair.

She drove to Galaxies. After checking with Jana, the receptionist, to ascertain Lucas's whereabouts and time of return, she went straight to Rick's office.

Methodically she checked his In and Out baskets, his dated memo file, his desk drawers, all the nooks and crannies of his credenza and his bookcase. His daily calendar proved to be a gold mine of information. There were names of people he'd had meetings with, phone numbers of tennis partners, friends and business associates, names of restaurants where he'd had lunch or after-work drinks. She jotted them all down in her ever-present notebook, then picked up the phone and called Sherri.

Rick's widow answered on the sixth ring. "Hello?" she said hesitantly.

"Hi, Sherri, it's Natalie Bishop. I don't mean to bother you, but—"

"Oh, no. No, you're not bothering me at all," she replied, sounding relieved. "I thought you might be one of those collection-agency people."

"Are you getting more calls?"

"All the time. I had no idea Ricky owed so many people so much money. It's getting so I'm afraid to answer the phone."

"You don't have to take their calls, you know."

"I don't?"

"No, you don't. There are strict laws about what a collection agency can and cannot do. Harassing people at home is one of the things they can't do."

"But . . . I don't know . . . I mean, how do I stop it?"

"Do you have a lawyer, Sherri?"

"Well, there's Mr. Kemp. He handled Ricky's will."

"No, I mean do *you* have a lawyer. Someone you like and can trust to help you sort this mess out?" Natalie knew even as she asked the question that the other woman didn't. "Look. I'd planned to stop by, anyway. I'd like to take a look around Rick's den if you don't mind. Why don't I bring the names of a couple of lawyers with me?"

"I don't know. . . ."

"I know you don't want to hear this, Sherri, but you're going to have to handle this whole mess sooner or later. And the longer you wait, the harder and more complicated it's going to get."

A long sigh came over the wire. "That's what Lucas said."

"He did?"

"Yes. He said he'd help me all he could, but that I was going to have to make some decisions on my own, and that I might just have to face the fact that bankrup—" she stumbled over the word as if it were completely unfamiliar "—bankruptcy might be my only choice. I suggested he might take care of all that for me, but he said I was going to have to learn to stand on my own two feet sometime."

"He did?"

"Yes, he did." She sighed. "So I guess I'd appreciate the names of those lawyers." She sounded years older than she had just a moment before.

Natalie took her the lawyers' names and numbers, as well as Andrea's, in case Sherri wanted to talk to a woman who'd been there and lived to tell about it. She left carrying a recent snapshot of Rick.

She took the photo and the mug shot of Marty Dobbs to the restaurant where Rick had most frequently had lunch, and asked bartenders, waiters and waitresses if they remembered seeing either of the two men. Nobody had. Then she went down to the Lamplighter's neighborhood, keeping a lookout for Cal or any of his bar buddies, and asked the neighboring businesses and the women working the street if they'd ever seen Rick before, and under what circumstances. She called Rick's tennis partner, catching him just before he left his office for the day. From him, she got an earful—not only about Rick's tennis-playing abilities, but about his college career, as well. He and his doubles partner had belonged to the same fraternity.

Rick's gambling was, apparently, nothing new. He'd gotten into trouble a couple of times, gambling too heavily on college games. His mother had bailed him out. There'd also been some sort of dustup about a test he may or may not have been caught cheating on, but Barbara had smoothed that over, too.

"His old lady donated a bundle for a new lab or something," the tennis partner told Natalie. "And nobody ever said another thing about the crib sheets they supposedly found on him."

Natalie sat in her car, frowning at the phone, wondering why Rick hadn't gone to his mother for help this last time. He'd needed her much more desperately than

he had before. Suddenly, the reason was clear to her.
She'd known at the first mention of a loan from Lucas,
on the day of Rick's funeral, that Rick had been trying
to cut the apron strings. Instinctively, she knew he'd
been trying to be his own man, trying to prove to himself that he could stand on his own two feet and make
a success of his life without any help or interference
from his mother.

Apparently he'd been unwilling, or unable, to make
the sacrifices necessary to follow through. He'd been
unwilling to change his life-style; unwilling, perhaps,
to risk losing his wife's blind adoration by asking for her
help. He'd forgotten—or maybe he'd never known—
that marriage was supposed to be a partnership. Two
people in love were supposed to depend on each other,
to help each other, to trust each other. He hadn't trusted
Sherri, obviously. He hadn't been willing to give her the
benefit of the doubt, hadn't—

Just the way, Natalie realized, she hadn't been willing to trust the man she loved.

The thought came without fanfare or surprise; it had
been sitting there, on the edge of her mind, waiting until she was ready to acknowledge it. It wasn't just an irresistible "lech" she felt for Lucas; it was love. She was
hopelessly, irrevocably in love with exactly the kind of
man she'd sworn never to get involved with.

But was he really that kind of man?

Oh, he looked macho enough to stop a tank with one
steely glance. He swaggered like a Marine in full pa-
rade dress. He might even actually think he believed all
that tripe about a woman needing masculine care and

guidance. But had he ever, even once, treated her with anything other than the respect due an equal?

Oh, sure, he had the unfortunate tendency to confuse her gender and lack of stature with the inability to look after herself, but that, on reflection, was a rather endearing quality. Annoying, maybe, but endearing. The important thing was . . . Had he ever talked down to her? Had he ever suggested, by word or deed, that he thought her opinions were worth less than his because she was a woman?

Not once that she could remember.

Which meant she'd gone and done what she was always accusing men of doing; she'd let herself be misled by the packaging. Because he looked mean and macho and dangerously sexy, conforming to her image of a backward, unenlightened male, she'd judged him at face value.

So, who was the sexist?

She slumped down behind the wheel and covered her eyes with her hand, fairly certain that the only sexist involved in their relationship was herself. If they still *had* a relationship after this morning . . . If they'd ever had a relationship.

"Don't be stupid," she said to herself, straightening behind the wheel. "Of course, we have a relationship. I hope."

She started the car and headed back toward the Galaxies office, eager to confront her lover and find out exactly what kind of relationship they had.

DESPITE THE FACT that it was seven o'clock on Friday night, all the parking spots directly in front of the Galaxies offices were full. Lucas's Jeep was there, parked between Daniel's beat-up van and, to her surprise, her father's unmarked police car.

Sensing trouble, Natalie parked her Ford and hurried into the building. Her father and Lucas were standing with their backs to the door, leaning over something or someone in the straight-backed chair next to the receptionist's desk.

"What's going on?" She tapped her father on the back to make him move. "Dad? What's— Oh, my God! Daniel!" She reached out as if to touch him and then dropped her hand, afraid even the gentle pressure of her fingers would cause him more pain. His right eye was swollen shut, and a blue-green bruise was already spreading down onto the curve of his left cheek. He held a bloody handkerchief pressed to his nose. "What happened to you?" she demanded.

Lucas answered for him. "Your friend from the Lamplighter paid him a little visit."

"My friend?"

"The amorous one with the crew cut and the beefy arms."

"You mean Cal beat him up? Oh, my God!" She reached out and, very gently, touched her brother's unbruised cheek. "He beat you up?"

Daniel held the handkerchief away from his nose so he could talk. "He only hit me a couple of times, Nat," he said thickly. "Dat hardly qualifies as a beating."

"But why?" She turned her head to look at Lucas, guilt in every line of her body. "Because of me? Did he beat Daniel up because of last night?"

"I doubt it," Lucas reassured her. "Unless you told him who you are, there was no way for him to make a connection."

"But then—" she motioned toward Daniel's battered face "—why?"

"He said he was delivering a message from Marty Dobbs," Lucas explained. "Isn't that right, Daniel?"

Daniel nodded.

"A message?" Natalie looked back and forth between her brother and her lover. "You mean he's trying to get the money Rick owes him out of Daniel?"

"That'd be my guess."

"But that's not—"

"What I'd like to know, little girl," her father interrupted, "was how the goon who beat up your brother came to be a friend of yours in the first place."

"Lucas didn't tell you?" She looked at Lucas.

"I thought you'd want to tell him yourself."

"Well, somebody sure as hell better tell me, and soon. Or I'm gonna haul both your butts in for obstruction of justice."

"I didn't obstruct anything, Dad. I, ah—" She knew he wasn't going to like it. "I merely went down to the Lamplighter last night and—"

"I knew it!" He looked at Lucas, a man-to-man, confirming-the-little-girl's-idiocy look. "Didn't I tell you? I knew she was gonna go down there." He looked back at his daughter. "Got yourself into trouble, didn't you?"

"No, I did not get myself into trouble," she retorted, shooting a look at Lucas that warned him to keep his mouth shut.

Unfortunately, her father caught the look. "What happened?" he demanded in his most official police-officer voice.

Natalie sighed. "I went into the Lamplighter and told the bartender I was looking for some action and—"

Her father grunted. "Probably thought you were a hooker."

Lucas snickered, quickly changing it to a cough as Natalie turned to glare at him.

"Nobody thought I was a hooker," she said firmly. "I told the bartender I'd heard Marty Dobbs handled his action out of the Lamplighter and I'd like to see him. So he called this Cal character over and—"

"That'd be Calvin Maloney." Her father nodded. "Dobbs's muscle."

"Our two-fisted friend." Lucas nodded at Daniel.

"One," Daniel corrected. "He only hit me with one hand."

The three men grinned at each other.

"Anyway—" Natalie gave them all a stern look to let them know this wasn't an occasion for any silly male bonding "—Cal said I'd have to talk to him before I could talk to his boss and—" She hesitated, knowing this was going to be the part her father would misunderstand the same way Lucas had. "We were having a slight . . . discussion over what the talk would entail, when Lucas showed up."

"He had her up against the bar," Lucas clarified. "And no one was doing a damned thing to stop him."

"He hurt you, Natalie?" Nathan demanded.

"Yes," Lucas replied.

"No," Natalie answered at the same time.

"Natalie Catherine?"

"So, he had me pushed up against the bar. I had my gun pressed against his ribs. I'd say things were about even at that point."

"I want you to come down to the station tomorrow and fill out a report."

"There's nothing to fill out a report about," Natalie objected. "Nothing happened."

"You pulled a gun on him."

"But I didn't shoot."

Father and daughter glared at each other for a full five seconds.

"Oh, hell," Nathan said finally, verbally throwing up his hands. He turned to his son. "You'll come down to the station and fill out a report about what happened here," he said sternly, as if, having lost one argument to an offspring, he wasn't about to lose another. "As soon as you feel up to it."

"I don't feel too bad right now, actually."

"You will later tonight," Lucas warned, grinning. "Your adrenaline's keeping you from feeling much right now, but in a little while your whole face will be throbbing. I'd recommend a couple of prescription pain pills if you have them, otherwise extra-strength aspirin and an ice pack."

"Shouldn't he see a doctor?" Natalie asked.

"What for? Nothing's broken."

"You know that for a fact, I suppose, Dr. Sinclair?"

"I've had my own nose broken enough times to know."

"Still—"

"Don't fuss, Nat. I'll be fine."

"Well, if that's all settled, I've got to get going." Nathan touched his son lightly on the shoulder. "I don't want you working here by yourself after hours until we get this thing cleared up."

"But, Dad—"

"No buts. Next time, that goon might hit you with more than one hand. You understand me?"

Daniel nodded.

Nathan looked over at his daughter. "That goes double for you, little girl," he said sternly. "No hanging around here by yourself, you got that? And stay the hell away from the Lamplighter." He nodded at Lucas. "Watch your back."

"Will do, sir."

Natalie watched her father out the door, then turned to look up at Lucas. He looked uncommonly determined about something, all of a sudden. "What is it?"

"What's what?"

"That look on your face. It—"

"Probably worry lines forming," he said, turning his attention back to Daniel. "How're you feeling?" He put his hand on the younger man's shoulder. "Pain kicked in yet?"

"Some."

"Why don't you take your brother home, Natalie? Tuck him into bed. Make him nice and comfortable. He's going to need a little TLC."

"And what are you going to do?"

He motioned toward his brother's old office. "I've got a few more things I want to look into here before I call it a night."

"Alone?"

"Why, Natalie—" he grinned in a way calculated to annoy her "—are you worried about me?"

"Not any more than I would be about anyone else who's determined to put themselves in danger," she lied.

"Well, don't. The message has been delivered." He nodded toward Daniel. "Dobbs'll give it a day or two before he comes calling for his answer. Go on." He motioned her toward her brother. "Take Daniel home and put him to bed. I'll lock up here."

Natalie looked up at him, unable to stop herself from asking the question: "You promise you're not in any danger?"

"Word of a Marine. Now go. Daniel's about to fall off that chair. And I've got a few calls to make." He turned away, disappearing into Rick's old office.

"I'll need to get some things from my workroom before we go," Daniel said. "And I want to hook up my modem so I can work from home." He got to his feet and headed toward his office. "I'll need to make extra copies of all the disks for the new game I've been working on," he muttered, mostly to himself. "And the graphs. I'll need the graphs." He glanced back over his shoulder. "Natalie?"

"I'll be there in a minute," she said, her eyes on the door Lucas had closed behind him. She'd have given half her collection of shoes to know who those "few calls" were going out to. There had to be a way to find out.

She turned, eyeing the blinking light on the telephone sitting on the receptionist's desk. She reached out, her fingers hovering over the buttons. Three lines, one of which he was using. What if— No, he'd hear the click if she picked up. Very gently, she pushed the intercom button instead, and hoped for the best.

"Eager as you are to get this settled," she heard Lucas say. "The sooner, the better."

There was a moment of silence.

"Now," Lucas said. "Ten minutes from now. Later tonight. You name it."

More silence.

"That won't be necessary. My brother kept real thorough records. Yeah—" His pleasant tone sounded evil to Natalie's ears. "I thought that might interest you."

Another fifteen seconds of silence ensued, during which Natalie would have given her *entire* collection of shoes to hear what Dobbs was saying. She *knew* it was Dobbs. It couldn't be anyone else.

"Here would be okay by me," she heard Lucas reply. "Yeah, ten o'clock. I'll be waiting."

12

NATALIE'S FIRST IMPULSE was to storm into the office in a blind fury and demand to know what the hell he thought he was doing, arranging to meet murderers behind her back. Her second impulse was more reasonable. Knowing Lucas would just deny everything and then arrange his meeting for another time, she decided a little discretion might be in order. As things stood right now, she at least knew when and where and, she thought, who.

He was meeting Marty Dobbs, making him think he had something to trade or bargain with. *My brother kept real thorough records,* he'd said, as if he had incriminating evidence of some sort.

Not a bad idea, actually, Natalie reflected. She'd give Lucas credit for that. Not a bad idea at all. But it *was* stupid for him to think he could carry it off alone.

Dobbs certainly wasn't going to be alone, no matter what he'd agreed to over the telephone. He'd bring his muscle-bound guard dog with him. Well, Lucas was going to have muscle, too, whether he wanted it or not. He was going to have her.

She released the intercom button very carefully and backed out of the reception area toward her brother's workroom, ready at any moment to reverse her steps to make it look as if she were just coming from that direction if Lucas opened his door.

He didn't.

Letting out a breath, Natalie ducked into Daniel's office. "You about ready?"

"Yeth," he said, sounding like a kid with a bad head cold. "I just need you to help me with some of this stuff."

"Give it here." She took an untidy stack of paper from him, tucking it securely into the crook of her arm, and took his elbow in her other hand. "Let's get you home before you keel over."

She got him into the front seat of her car, stashed his gear in the back, then went back inside to get her purse and let Lucas know they were leaving. She pounded on his closed office door. "Lucas, I'm taking Daniel—" the door opened abruptly, causing her to stumble against him "—home now," she said into his chest. She put a hand up to push herself away.

He put his hand on top of it, holding her where she was. "It might be a good idea if you spent the night at his place," Lucas told her. "He may wake up and need something."

"Maybe I'll do that," she agreed mendaciously, standing eye-to-unblinking-eye with the cobra on the back of his hand. The sight was slightly unnerving. And exciting. It reminded her of all the lovely things that hand had done to her last night.

This isn't the time, she told herself sternly, and tried to draw her hand from beneath his.

His fingers tightened. "Natalie?"

She looked up. "What?"

"Just this." He wrapped his other arm around her and, yanking her up against him, he planted a very thorough, very possessive kiss on her half-open mouth.

Natalie tried very hard not to be thrilled by it.

"I'll see you tomorrow," he said, very seriously. "We have a lot to talk about."

"We certainly do," she replied, withdrawing from his embrace and thinking, *We'll talk a lot sooner than tomorrow!*

NATALIE GOT HER BROTHER home and into bed with an ice bag over his closed eye and swollen cheek, and left him snoring softly, despite his protests that he had far too much work left to do on his latest video game to waste time sleeping. Then she went home and changed into a pair of skinny black jeans, a plain black blouse and a pair of 5AA black sneakers, which she wore as seldom as possible because they added no height. Finally, she added the shoulder holster her father had given her when he'd grudgingly presented her with the .38 revolver. Its tan leather was a little stiff from being so seldom worn, but the holster fit snugly under her left arm, invisible to the untrained eye beneath her unstructured black silk jacket. She slipped the gun in and out of the holster a few times, making sure it didn't catch on anything, then went to the phone and dialed her father.

She'd given it a good deal of thought on the drive from Daniel's apartment to her house and had decided she wanted more people on hand to protect Lucas—just in case. There was no telling how dangerous Dobbs really was. And he was certain to bring along Calvin Maloney, which meant there was no telling how violently Lucas would react.

She remembered vividly the look Lucas had given the beefy muscle-man in the bar. It was a look that said he wasn't going to be satisfied with just one knockout punch; it had said he wasn't going to be satisfied with anything less than a serious attempt to rearrange her attacker's face. Quite honestly, she didn't trust Lucas to have enough self-control to refrain from doing just that at the first opportunity.

Her father wasn't available.

She left a message, telling the officer who answered she'd try again, and sat down to wait. It wouldn't be dark until at least eight-thirty, maybe nine, and she needed the cover of darkness. The same was true, she was sure, for Marty Dobbs; that's why he'd chosen ten in the evening for his meeting. The night covered a multitude of misdeeds.

At eight forty-five, she called her father again, with the same results. She hesitated a moment, then shrugged philosophically and headed out to her car. A backup of one was better than no backup at all.

She arrived at the office park just before nine o'clock and parked behind the building, where her car was well hidden among some repair trucks from another business. On foot, she made her way around the side of the building until she had a clear view of Galaxies's front doors. Lucas's black Jeep and Daniel's beat-up van were the only two vehicles in the entire parking lot. Satisfied that Dobbs hadn't arrived yet, Natalie crept back around the building and quietly unlocked the rear door of Galaxies.

Slipping inside, she stood with her back against the door for a moment or two, letting her eyes adjust to the darkness, listening for the slightest sound. It was deathly quiet, but fortunately, not completely dark. Light from the front corner office, where she assumed Lucas was waiting, spilled out into the hallway, providing her with enough light to make out the shapes of office furniture and video machines.

She crept forward quietly, a careful step at a time, until finally she reached the receptionist's desk, thinking the kneehole underneath would be the perfect place to hide. She would be completely hidden from view unless someone came around behind the desk and crouched down to look. In the exceedingly unlikely event that someone did just that—she patted the revolver tucked under her arm—she was ready.

Less than thirty minutes later, but still a full twenty minutes early by her calculations, Natalie heard footsteps—but not coming in from the outside. Lucas, she decided, stepping out of his office. Everything was quiet again for a moment, and then the front door opened and someone came in.

Just one someone? she wondered, discovering the single disadvantage of her hiding place. She couldn't be seen, but neither could she see. She held her breath, straining to hear.

"Hello?" The unfamiliar voice echoed through the empty offices. "Anyone here?"

"Dobbs?" Lucas's voice came from a corner of the reception area, well back in the shadows.

She heard the carpet whisper as someone—Marty Dobbs?—abruptly turned. "Lucas Sinclair?" There was a pause and then: "There was no need to set the stage quite so dramatically, Mr. Sinclair," the unfamiliar voice said. "As you can see, I'm alone."

Natalie heard the creak of the front door opening and closing again as, presumably, Lucas checked outside. "Just making sure."

A light went on.

"You don't look much like your brother," Marty Dobbs observed.

"We're only half brothers."

"And you're much older than he was."

"I'm his older half brother." Lucas's voice was tinged with careless sarcasm. Natalie was amazed at how different he sounded. *Rough* and *uneducated* were the only words that came to her mind.

"I wonder why he never mentioned you? Poor Ricky and I got to be very . . . close during our association."

"Yeah; I'll bet." Natalie could hear the thinly veiled impatience in the rough response. "Look, Dobbs, we're not here to discuss your association with 'poor Ricky.' We're here to make a deal. So cut the crap."

"Not at all like poor Ricky," Dobbs repeated. "That young man was unfailingly polite."

"He's also dead."

"An unfortunate accident," Dobbs said carelessly. "He was only supposed to be scared into a more timely payment plan."

"He owed me twenty thousand dollars when you ar- ranged for him to kiss that wall at sixty miles an hour."

"Oh, so that was you, was it?" Dobbs said calmly, neither denying nor confirming Lucas's accusation. "He made a twenty-thousand-dollar installment on his debt—last January, I believe it was. I wondered who'd lent him the money. He said his mother wouldn't."

"The old broad's obviously a lot smarter than me," Lucas replied. "She probably knew he was just talkin' through his hat about this hotshot company of his."

"It's not all he said it was, then?"

"Hell no. He gave me this big song and dance about how him and that partner of his had the 'biggest com- puter thing since the Nintendo game' about ready to hit the market. It was gonna make millions, he said. And all he needed was a little cash to tide him over until it was finished. I was gonna make back at least ten times my investment. Twenty if it went as big as he thought it would. Hell," Lucas fumed, amazing Natalie with both his acting skill and his inventiveness, "this com- pany ain't nothin' but a two-bit operation. Does okay, I suppose. Or would, if my 'polite' little brother hadn't been skimming the profits all along. But a two-bit op- eration isn't good enough for me. I don't have the pa- tience for it."

"And that's where I come in."

"Yeah," Lucas said, his tone such that Natalie didn't have to concentrate very hard to imagine the cynical expression and gunslinger stance that went with it. "That's where you come in."

"I suppose you want me to give you your twenty thousand back?"

"You're thinkin' the right way," Lucas confirmed, "but not the right amount."

Silence was his only answer.

"I want two hundred thousand."

Natalie nearly swallowed her tongue. Two hundred thousand dollars? What in heaven's name was Lucas trying to do?

"In exchange for?" Marty Dobbs asked calmly.

"Like I said on the phone. Rick kept thorough records. Real thorough records, if you get my drift. He was what you might call a compulsive list maker. Wrote everything down. Dates, amounts, spread, payoffs. There's even a real interesting list of some of your other clients. Real pillars of the community, some of them," Lucas continued, embellishing what was actually there until it sounded, even to Natalie, as if he really had something worth bargaining for. "He wrote down all the threats you made against him, too."

Under the desk, Natalie wondered if Lucas had gone too far. Writing down threats?

"I never make threats, Mr. Sinclair." Marty Dobbs's voice was suddenly very, very cold. "I make promises. And I'll make you a promise right now. You give me those records you say your brother kept and I'll let you walk out of here alive."

Under the desk, Natalie shivered, remembering having wondered about Dobbs's capacity for violence, and thinking now that anyone who could sound like that had a very great capacity, indeed, for coldhearted mayhem. *Watch him, Lucas!* she silently warned. *Watch him.*

"As soon as you hand over the two hun—"

There was a sharp thud, a muffled grunt, and then the sound of a body hitting the floor.

Natalie went very still in her hidey-hole, every muscle in her body straining as she listened for the next sound, the next voice. What was going on? Who'd been hit? Who'd grunted? Whose body had hit the floor?

Please, God, she prayed, *please don't let it be Lucas.* But she was very much afraid that it was.

"What the hell—" Calvin Maloney's tone was surprised. "This is the guy from the bar. The one who . . . uh . . ."

"Nearly took your head off?" his boss said smoothly.

"He sucker punched me," Cal defended himself. "He wouldn't of had a chance except for that woman."

"Ah, yes. The woman. I wonder how she fits in to all of this?"

"You want I should find out?" Cal said eagerly.

The silent answer must have been yes, Natalie thought despairingly, because there was the awful sound of a blow being struck followed immediately by a grunt of pain.

Natalie mashed her fingers to her lips to keep from crying out. *Keep cool,* she told herself, fighting an almost overwhelming fear for the man she loved. *Keep cool and wait.* The right opportunity to save them both would present itself if she just kept her cool!

There was another thud—*God, was he kicking Lucas?*—another grunt.

Why wasn't Lucas fighting back? And where the hell was her father when she needed him? Didn't he ever check in for messages?

"That's enough, Cal," Dobbs ordered sharply.

Natalie could have kissed his feet.

"I owe him," Cal snarled.

"I understand your frustration." Dobbs's voice was smoothly sympathetic. "But restrain yourself for the time being. I need him to show me where those records are and tell me how that woman is involved. When I have them you can arrange another little accident like the one you did for poor Ricky." His voice hardened. "Get him on his feet."

There was a long moment of silence. A thud. A grunt. "Get the hell up, Sinclair. Before I really hurt you."

Natalie couldn't stand it another second. She couldn't cower under the desk and let that thug beat Lucas to a bloody pulp. And the only way an opportunity was going to show itself was if she made one. She crept out on all fours, quickly but cautiously, and peered around the edge of the desk. She found herself at eye level with the backs of a pair of legs clad in expensive tan slacks.

Marty Dobbs, in the flesh.

This was going to be easy.

She started to slide her hand under the lapel of her jacket, reaching for her gun, when her gaze shifted beyond the tan slacks to see Lucas, half crouched over, weaving unsteadily on his feet. Cal Maloney stood behind him with a gun held, muzzle first like a club, in his hand, and a smile of pure evil on his face. A trickle of blood oozed over the curve of Lucas's neck, staining the collar of his shirt.

For a wild moment Natalie actually considered rushing forward like an outraged pit bull and sinking her teeth into the hand holding the gun, gleefully anticipating the howl of outrage and the copious flow of blood. She calmed herself, curling her hand around the butt of the revolver under her jacket, and telling herself to wait . . . to wait for just the right moment. Cal or Lucas or both of them would move, and then she would have a clear shot at the bastard. But then Cal punched Lucas in the small of the back and laughed as he staggered.

Natalie went completely berserk and forgot everything she'd ever learned about coolness under fire. Uttering a scream of pure, unadulterated rage, she surged to her feet, clipping Marty Dobbs as she rose so that he staggered to one side, and launched her entire one hundred two pounds of screaming female fury at Cal Maloney's chest. She caught him off balance, knocking the loosely held gun from his hand, sending them both careening into the wall.

And then all hell broke loose.

Someone grabbed her from behind—Marty Dobbs, she guessed—and flung her away from her intended victim, depriving her of the satisfaction of sinking her nails into his flesh. She hit the floor and rolled, coming right back to her feet, fully intending to fling herself into the fray on behalf of her gravely injured beloved.

"For Chrissake, Natalie, get the hell out of the way!" Lucas roared, shouldering her aside.

And then she was grabbed again and pulled roughly back. And this time it *was* Marty Dobbs. He held her with his hands around her biceps, keeping her arms at her sides, but so loosely she was half aware he didn't consider her much of a threat. The other half of her mind was focused on the sight of Lucas. He was on his feet! A little wobbly, maybe, but on his feet. His heavy boxer's shoulders were hunched, flexing and coiling as he landed blows with the precision of a machine. Natalie felt like screaming like a fan at a boxing match.

Then she saw the gun she'd knocked out of Cal Maloney's hand. It was lying on the floor between her and the two men who were presently trying to beat each other to a bloody pulp. She realized that Marty Dobbs had seen the gun, too, and was slowly dragging her toward it.

She brought her heel down on top of Dobbs's foot with vicious intent, twisting it in a grinding motion, expecting to hear a howl of pain as she was let free. She was amazed when it brought only a grunt and a sharp slap to the side of her head.

No heels, she remembered, and began struggling furiously, trying to twist her arms out of his grasp so she could grab her gun. He shook her like a rag doll, snapping her head back and forth, and then his forearm went around her throat, cutting off her air.

She quit reaching for her gun and grabbed at his arm instead, gasping for oxygen.

"Let go," he hissed in her ear. "Let go."

She let go, coughing and choking, and he immediately loosened his hold, just slightly, so she could breathe.

"That's a good girl," he said in her ear. "Good girl. Now move with me," he ordered, forcing her closer to the gun on the floor. "That's it."

She sidestepped with him, obedient and whimpering softly for effect. It worked. He underestimated her again and loosened his hold, starting to lean sideways to pick up the gun.

Natalie reached under her jacket and yanked her revolver out of the holster. Too late, he realized what she'd done and tried to knock it out of her hand. She jerked her arm down and away, avoiding his grasp.

The gun went off.

"Bitch!" Dobbs howled and let her go.

"I'm all right," she screamed to Lucas, afraid the gunfire would distract him and give Cal some kind of advantage. "I'm all right."

She swung around as she spoke, the gun in her hands, and pointed it directly between Marty Dobbs's wide-spaced bulging eyes. "Move and I'll kill you," she said, meaning it with every fiber of her being.

He froze, half crouched, one hand extended inches from the gun on the floor.

"Maybe I'll just shoot you in the kneecaps," Natalie threatened, lowering the muzzle of the gun slightly, daring him to move.

He looked at the gun, then up into her eyes. Then, very slowly, Marty Dobbs straightened.

"Back up," Natalie ordered. "Go on, back up. Against the wall. Turn around and assume the position." She gestured with the gun. "I'm sure you know it."

She waited until he'd done as she said, then pushed her glasses up on her nose and glanced down, looking for the other gun. It was right by her foot. She crouched down, never taking her eyes—or her own gun—off Dobbs, and picked it up. "You about done there?" she asked Lucas over her shoulder.

"Just . . . about," he managed. He grabbed Maloney by the back of his shirt with both hands and ran him, face first, into the wall. The man crumpled without a sound.

Suddenly the police burst through both the front and back doors, just as Lucas grunted and fell back against the wall himself, panting like a winded bull.

"It's about time you showed up," Natalie exclaimed, scowling at her father. "I was beginning to wonder if you got my message."

"What the hell message is that, little girl?" Nathan motioned for Coffey to take care of Dobbs and reached out to take Maloney's gun from his daughter. "We were in the back of Daniel's truck, providing backup for Lucas, here."

Natalie started to slip her own gun back into its shoulder holster. "Providing backup?"

Her father wagged his fingers at her. "Give it here," he told her, meaning the gun. "Ballistics is gonna want to go over it."

Natalie handed it over.

"Did you get enough?" Lucas demanded, pushing away from the wall as Officer Larson bent to retrieve the limp form of Calvin Maloney.

"Enough," Nathan grunted, watching his daughter take Lucas Sinclair's bloody hand in hers. She slipped her other arm around his waist, and gently set her shoulder into his armpit to offer support.

"Unless all that screaming Natalie did wiped it all out," Coffey remarked as he steered the handcuffed, limping Dobbs toward the front door; her wild shot had hit him in the foot. "Practically broke my eardrum," Coffey added, frowning at her.

"What's he talking about?" Natalie demanded, looking back and forth between her father and Lucas as she steered the latter toward the desk.

"Our boy here is wired for sound," Nathan replied.

"Wired for—?" She fixed her father with a steely gaze. "You mean you were in on this harebrained stunt?" she asked incredulously. "You agreed to help him get himself killed?"

"The only harebrained stunt I've seen tonight was masterminded by you," Lucas said before Nathan could answer. "I've never seen anything so damned stupid in my life!" He eased himself down onto the edge of the desk as Natalie slipped out from under his arm. "You jumping out from behind the desk like a screaming Valkyrie bent on wholesale destruction. And without the slightest idea what you were getting into!"

"Me!" she scoffed, reaching out to unbutton his shirt as if he were a child. "If I hadn't jumped out from behind this desk you'd be knocking on the devil's door right now because Cal Maloney would have kicked your brains out."

"If you hadn't been hiding behind that desk, I'd've never had to let Maloney *try* to kick my brains out!"

"Let him try—?" Her hands paused in their task. "You let him kick you?"

"What the hell else was I supposed to do when I saw you under that desk?"

"You saw me?"

"There's about a half inch of clearance under the desk when you're flat on your face on the floor. I could see your fanny and your little black sneakers." He smiled at her, a wry little half-smile that sent her heart tripping wildly. "No one else I know has feet that small." He reached up to touch her cheek. "I couldn't take the chance you'd get hurt."

"So you let yourself get beat up." She snorted inelegantly and resumed unbuttoning his shirt, needing action to stop the tears she could feel perilously close to the surface at his unexpectedly tender action. "That makes a whole hell of a lot of sense."

"More sense than you trying to take Maloney out with a body check."

"He stopped kicking you, didn't he?" She parted his shirt, encountered the adhesive tape holding the tiny microphone and wires to his chest, and ripped them off.

"Ow-w! Jeez, Natalie, take it easy."

"What's the matter?" she asked, thrusting the sound equipment at her father without taking her eyes off Lucas. "Does it hurt the big bad Marine?"

"Yes," he admitted, rubbing his chest where she'd pulled out hair. "It hurts." His hand drifted to his side. "All over."

Her eyes softened, losing some of their fire. "Does it?"

"Yes," he murmured, entranced by the look of loving concern in her face.

"Let me see." She reached out to push his blood-spattered shirt off his shoulders and ran her hands gently over his chest and sides. "Did he break any ribs?"

Nathan cleared his throat. "You want me to call a doctor?" he asked. Neither of them heard him. He grinned and backed out of the office, leaving them alone.

"Oh, Lucas." She touched the spreading bruise on his side with tender, loving fingers. "It looks awful. *You* look awful." He looked magnificent, actually. Bloody but unbowed. *My hero*, she thought, feeling just the slightest bit decadent for the heated way the sight of him made her feel, even now. "Are you in very much pain?"

"Some. But it looks worse than it feels," he lied, thoroughly enjoying being fussed over by the woman he loved.

"Does it?" She leaned forward and, very lightly and tenderly and infinitely lovingly, kissed his bruised ribs. "I wish I could do something to make it feel better," she said, kissing him again, this time on the spot where she'd pulled the adhesive tape off.

"You just did." He reached out and cupped her cheek, bringing her face up to his. "You were magnificent," he told her, staring into her eyes. "A pint-size Amazon warrior," he whispered. "But if you ever do anything like that again, I'm going to forget I was ever an officer and a gentleman and paddle your butt until you can't sit down for a week. Is that clear?"

"You and what army?" she challenged.

He laughed, but softly, careful of the pain in his side. "You just don't know when to quit, do you?"

She pressed his hand against her cheek and then took it in both of hers, turning it so the back, with its coiled cobra and bleeding knuckles, was between them. "Do you?" she asked, and kissed those wounds, too.

"If I knew what was good for me, I'd quit right now." Very carefully, he disengaged his hand from hers and put his arms around her. Drawing her to him, he spread his knees to bring her close. "But, obviously, I don't. Know when to quit, that is. I do know what's good for me, though," he added. "Finally."

She looped her arms around his neck, resting them lightly on his broad shoulders. "And what's that?" she whispered, so close her lips brushed against his when she spoke.

"You," he whispered back.

"You sure?"

"Positive." He rubbed his cheek against the exquisite softness of hers. "And I know what's good for you, too."

"You would," Natalie agreed dryly, returning his nuzzling with some nuzzling of her own. "What?"

"What what?"

"What's good for me?"

"I am," he said, drawing back slightly in an effort to gauge her reaction to his pronouncement. They were eye to eye, lip to lip, breathing each other's air—and loving it.

"We fight nearly all the time," she reminded him, just to see what he would say.

"We engage in a spirited exchange of ideas."

"And I'm really not your type. You said so yourself."

"I was obviously mistaken."

"And you don't really like me."

"Now, that's true."

Natalie furrowed her brow at him.

"I don't just like you," he clarified. "I love you." He grinned. "God help me."

She smiled beatifically. "I was hoping you felt that way, because I love you, too." Her grin matched his. "God help us both."

"Amen," Lucas said and kissed her. Thoroughly.

"So," Natalie continued when she could, "what are we going to do about it?"

"Being in love?"

Natalie nodded.

"Get married," Lucas answered, as if it were the only option. And as far as he was concerned, it was.

Natalie looked thoughtful. "Do you really think that's a good idea, Lucas? I mean, really?" She spoke seriously, as if she actually had a legitimate objection, instead of just the desire to let him know he was being insufferably autocratic again. "Not that I don't love you. I do. Desperately. But we're not at all alike. Maybe we should just live together for a while and see how it goes."

"We're getting married."

"But we haven't got anything in common—not really—and—"

"Just the important things." He cupped her buttocks, pressing her against the cleft of his open thighs to emphasize the point.

"There's more to life than incredible sex."

Lucas grinned. "Incredible, huh?"

Natalie frowned at him. "Don't try to change the subject," she said sternly. "We were discussing whether or not we should get married or just live to—"

"We're getting married," Lucas declared masterfully. "Period. End of discussion. Now shut up, you contrary witch, and kiss me."

Natalie decided, just this once—because he was undoubtedly in pain and probably didn't know how arrogant he sounded, and she didn't really feel like arguing anyway—to let him get away with ordering her around.

She shut up and kissed him.

Thoroughly.

Epilogue

"AND JUST WHERE do you think you're going?" Lucas demanded of his wife.

Natalie pretended she hadn't heard him and pushed open one side of the double glass doors of the spacious suite of offices. Bold gold lettering on the glass listed the names Galaxies Video, Strictly Confidential Investigations and Sinclair Security Systems.

"Natalie," Lucas said, reaching out to grasp her by the shoulder. "I asked you where you were going."

Natalie turned to look at him. "I believe we had this discussion earlier this morning," she replied, her expression clearly letting him know how close to exasperated she was.

"And we decided you weren't going."

"No. *You* decided I wasn't going. I merely didn't bother to disagree. Now, if you'll excuse me—" she looked pointedly at the large hand still resting on her shoulder "—I have a suspected arson to investigate."

"I forbid it."

Natalie's eyebrows rose into her wispy blond bangs. "Forbid it?" she repeated coolly, her brown eyes snapping.

"Oh, hell." He dropped his hand and tried to look sheepish and unthreatening, with limited success. Men as large and macho as Lucas rarely succeeded in looking unthreatening. "It's for your own good." He looked to the blue-suited woman standing in front of the filing cabinet for help. "Tell her it's for her own good," he demanded.

Sherri Peyton laughed lightly and shook her red head. "Don't drag me into this, Lucas. I'm studying business administration, not family counseling." She closed the file drawer with her hip. "You're on your own, big fella."

Lucas turned back to his wife. "Dammit, Natalie, you're in no condition to go traipsing door-to-door, asking a lot of nosy questions about some poor sap's house fire. You know how easily you tire lately."

Some of Natalie's exasperation turned to fond indulgence at her husband's concern for her. "If I get tired, I'll rest, okay?"

Clearly unconvinced, he gave her a mulish look.

She sighed. "Lucas, I'm pregnant, not disabled. I'll be fine."

"And what if you go into labor or something?"

"At seven months?"

"It's been known to happen."

"To women with problem pregnancies. Which, if you'll remember what the doctor said the last time you started acting crazy, does not include me. I'm as healthy as the proverbial horse."

"You could fall," he argued, waving a hand toward the bright red shoes she wore. *Ridiculous footwear for a pregnant woman.* "Or turn an ankle."

"Not likely," she said, thinking with distaste of the sturdy, low-heeled pumps she'd worn only to counterbalance her protruding stomach. "And if I do, I'll scream for help. I'm not heading out into the wilds, you know," she teased. "I'll be within sight and sound of civilization at all times."

He folded his arms across his chest. "I still don't like it."

"I know you don't," she said soothingly.

"And yet you still insist on being unreasonable."

"I'm not the one being unreasonable here, Lucas. You're the one be— Never mind." She shook her head. "Okay, listen up, Sinclair. I'll make you a deal."

"I'm listening."

"With an open mind?" she questioned, eyeing his crossed arms.

He uncrossed them.

Natalie smiled. "What if I promise to go out for only half the time I intended. Say, just three hours? And then I'll go straight home and put my feet up for the rest of the day."

"In exchange for?" he asked. If there was one thing he'd learned about his wife in two years of marriage, it was that she didn't offer to compromise her maddeningly fierce independence for nothing.

"In exchange for you taking me to your mother's little cocktail party tomorrow night."

"Oh, no," he said, holding up his hands. "We've already discussed that. My mother and I have nothing to say to each other. Never have, never will."

"Obviously, she thinks differently." Natalie reached out and put her hand on her husband's arm. "This is her third attempt to make some kind contact with you, Lucas. And you've said yourself—more than once— that you might have judged her a little too harshly all those years ago. Maybe she feels the same way about you." She squeezed his arm gently. "As a future mother, I *know* she does," she added, placing her other hand on her rounded stomach. "I think she wants another chance, and I think you should at least meet her halfway."

Lucas eyed the hand on her belly. "You're not playing fair," he told her, reaching out to cover it with his own. The coiled cobra looked incongruous and, yet, somehow strangely right against the backdrop of fecund maternity.

Natalie smiled. "So you'll do it?"

Lucas sighed and gave in. "Only if you agree to cut your interviewing down to an hour."

"Two hours," she countered.

"All right." Lucas pushed open the door, motioning her to go through it, then followed her out. "Two hours, but I go with you."

"I don't need a watchdog, Lucas."

"It's that or nothing."

"You are the most pigheaded, stubborn..." The door swung closed behind them, and they continued arguing all the way to the car, trading familiar insults and accusations about the contrary ways of the other. But their hands were firmly clasped, and Lucas bent down to kiss his wife lingeringly before helping her into the black Jeep.

LOVE AND LAUGHTER

Look for:

Delightful, entertaining, steamy romps. All you expect from Harlequin Temptation—and humor, too!

SLIP BETWEEN THE COVERS...

NEW-1

HARLEQUIN *Temptation*

Rebels & Rogues

All men are not created equal. Some are rough around the edges. Tough-minded but tenderhearted. Incredibly sexy. The tempting fulfillment of every woman's fantasy.

When it's time to fight for what they believe in, to win that special woman, our Rebels and Rogues are heroes at heart.

Josh: He swore never to play the hero . . . unless the price was right.

THE PRIVATE EYE by Jayne Ann Krentz. Temptation #377, January 1992.

Matt: A hard man to forget . . . and an even harder man not to love.

THE HOOD by Carin Rafferty. Temptation #381, February 1992.

At Temptation, 1992 is the Year of Rebels and Rogues. Look for twelve exciting stories about bold and courageous men, one each month. Don't miss upcoming books from your favorite authors, including Candace Schuler, JoAnn Ross and Janice Kaiser.

Available wherever Harlequin books are sold.　RR-1

Harlequin
HISTORICAL

CHRISTMAS
STORIES · 1991

Bring back heartwarming memories of Christmas past,
with Historical Christmas Stories 1991, a collection of
romantic stories by three popular authors:

Christmas Yet To Come
by Lynda Trent
A Season of Joy
by Caryn Cameron
Fortune's Gift
by DeLoras Scott

A perfect Christmas gift!

1992

Celebrate the most romantic day of the year with
MY VALENTINE 1992—a sexy new collection of four
romantic stories written by our famous Temptation
authors:

> GINA WILKINS
> KRISTINE ROLOFSON
> JOANN ROSS
> VICKI LEWIS THOMPSON

My Valentine 1992—an exquisite escape into a romantic
and sensuous world.

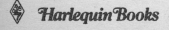

Harlequin Books

VAL-92-R

HARLEQUIN
PROUDLY PRESENTS
A DAZZLING NEW CONCEPT IN ROMANCE FICTION

One small town—twelve terrific love stories

Welcome to Tyler, Wisconsin—a town full of people
you'll enjoy getting to know, memorable friends and
unforgettable lovers, and a long-buried secret that
lurks beneath its serene surface....

JOIN US FOR A YEAR IN THE LIFE OF TYLER

Each book set in Tyler is a self-contained love story;
together, the twelve novels stitch the fabric of a
community.

LOSE YOUR HEART TO TYLER!

The excitement begins in March 1992, with
WHIRLWIND, by Nancy Martin. When lively, brash
Liza Baron arrives home unexpectedly, she moves
into the old family lodge, where the silent and
mysterious Cliff Forrester has been living in seclusion
for years....

WATCH FOR ALL TWELVE BOOKS OF THE TYLER SERIES
Available wherever Harlequin books are sold